A Geek,
An Angel

&

The Deceiver

BY
J.A. JACKSON

For Rossi, Daddy & Mommy always....

Acknowledgments

Special thanks to the incredible man in my life, my husband who believed in my writing. You are my best friend and the love of my life. Thank you WPC for the beginning of a fabulous journey.

Prologue

Eve Lafoy sighed heavily as thunder and lightning crisscrossed the sky. She watched eagerly as a faint radiance of rain danced on the car's windshield. In a few weeks the rains would make the brown, dry hills a deep green.

Sitting quietly, her thoughts preyed upon her. She bit her lip as she fought against the images trying to force their way into her mind. She burned with humiliation remembering that night. It had all started with a dare.

She remembered…The Grand Isles Christmas Ball 1993.

"My God, I hate this dress. Carina Sinclair rolled her eyes. "It's the last time I'm taking my mother with me to pick out a dress."

Eve Lafoy lifted a brow. "I told you it wasn't a good idea. *The Grand Isles* Christmas Ball is by far the biggest event of the year. And you trusted the dress you were to be seen in to your mother," Eve said, in a huff. "But you wouldn't listen to your best friend."

The *Grand Isles* annual Christmas Ball brought together all of the families who had come from Louisiana or had old family connections with the lustrous old state. Their main purpose was the debutante ball and to raise money for charity.

Carina adjusted her dress and sighed. "Do you want to go and get a glass of punch with me Evie?"

"Not now Carina."

Eve Lafoy had one thing in mind that night and it wasn't a glass of punch. She came to the party to dance with him.

"Why not?" Carina Sinclair asked.

Eve annoyingly breathed out, "Because we agreed tonight we are both drinking a glass of champagne."

Carina shrugged. "Look Evie, I prefer punch," she wrinkled up her nose. "This champagne tastes funny."

"That's because it's not the good stuff your parents buy for their parties."

Carina whined and took another sip. "Yuck! This stuff tastes terrible. You can have my glass. Why are you drinking this stuff anyway?"

Eve stared back at her.

"Oh! I almost forgot," Carina said in an excited voice. "Tonight's the night you're trying to get your courage up and ask Hawke Deville to dance with you, aren't you?"

Edwina Johnson squealed closing the distance between them. "I heard you. Say that wasn't the bet. The bet was you had to get him to kiss you Evie. Here, you'd better drink my glass of champagne. You'll need it."

"Don't call me Evie, Edwina Annie Mae Johnson," Eve snapped. "You wouldn't want me running around this debutante ball yelling Annie Mae at the top of my lungs, now would you?"

Edwina blinked rapidly. "No, no I wouldn't."

"Say, who invited you into the conversation, eavesdropper?" Carina snapped.

"Oh don't worry about her," Eve said taking Edwina's champagne. "Edwina can't even keep the bet straight in her own mind. I only have to dance with him."

Eve wished a big whole would just open up and swallow her. Carina and Edwina could argue all night about nothing.

"Whew," slowly Edwina breathed out, her eyes rapidly blinking nervously. "There he is! The man himself. Damn Hawke Deville is *man pretty*."

Carina snapped her head around. "Edwina there's no such word as *man pretty*. Hawke Deville is sexy, fine and handsome."

"Whatever Carina, Dawg you're like a dog with a bone sometimes," Edwina replied.

"And you're like that kid that's always hanging around your house just so they can steal something."

"Stop it you two, before someone gets their feelings hurt," Eve commanded.

Edwina coughed and cleared her throat. "Don't look now, I think he's coming this way."

All at once Eve swallowed the glass of champagne, arched her brow, straightened her shoulders, and glided over with an exaggerated sway of her hips and met Hawke Deville halfway. She leaned over and whispered in his ear.

Hawke Deville and Eve Lafoy walked to the dance floor.

"Damn, would you look at that?" Edwina Johnson exclaimed. "They are dancing so close. They only have eyes for each other."

"Pay up Edwina!"

"What?"

Carina snapped her head around and stared back. "You owe Edwina. Eve and I won the bet. She's dancing with Hawke. I want our money."

"Gee, don't get your panties all in a bunch. Follow me. I have to go and get my purse," Edwina said.

Carina looked back at Eve and waved to get her attention. She gave Eve a high five waive before strolling off with Edwina.

Funny, Eve thought, it was the last thing she remembered about that night. After that her inhibitions must have been lowered by the effects of the champagne. She remembered flinging herself into Hawke's arms, and with no regrets telling him that she loved him.

Even now she could feel her body responding just thinking about it.

That night had been so amazing and she felt warm and cozy when she woke up that morning. She rolled over and felt something warm.

She froze.

"Good morning Eve. So, did I take you to the sexual adventure of your life?"

"What?"

"I was your first, right?"

Eve blinked slowly. The meaning of what he was saying shot through her brain. "Oh my God, I was only supposed to kiss you."

Then she remembered. Eve stiffened at the shock of intimacy. Her heart started fluttering strangely.

Hawke lowered his head and pressed a hard kiss to her lips. He tasted her slowly and thoroughly. "There, now I've only kissed you."

He was a master kisser.

A knock sounded on Eve's bedroom door.

"Who is it?"

"Eve it's me Carina. Your mother is on her way upstairs right now. You'd better get Hawke out of your bedroom now."

"Oh my God Carina, what should I do with him?"

Carina shrugged. "Oh for goodness sake just hide him in your closet like all sixteen-year-old teenage girls do."

Chapter 1

Cars were lined up on both sides of the street of Skyline Boulevard. The neighborhood of stately mansions with majestic views of both Oakland and San Francisco bay skyline had long been the enclave of the elite and wealthy.

The mansion belonged to Xavier Newhouse. He was a self-made local business man and part owner of Newhouse Enterprises, a company that he'd owned with several of his cousins.

Carina Sinclair sighed slowly. "It's a good thing Xavier said I could park in the driveway. This street is packed full of cars."

"My God Carina, you drive slower than a turtle walks. We're late for the party," her best friend Eve Lafoy snapped.

Carina rolled her eyes. She could never get mad at Eve.

The first time she ever laid eyes on Eve she knew they would be best friends. To her Eve was an angel, a special gift sent from heaven to be Carina's best friend. "Oh quit being so bossy Evie."

Eve sighed heavily reaching into her purse for her compact. "Turn on the light. I want to fix my make-up."

Carina did as she was told. "You're lucky I was raised to respect my elders."

Eve touched up her mascara. "Too bad this elder didn't teach you how to drive faster. We would have been here a long time ago."

Carina sighed. "Evie Lafoy it was raining cats and dogs. What did you want me to do? Kill us both on the drive here?"

"Don't make jokes like that, they aren't funny Carina Sinclair. And do not call me Evie while we're at the party," a scowl marred her expression as she lifted her chin. "Call me Eve. It sounds so much more worldly and mature."

Carina made grunting noises. "Aw you make me want to start drinking sometimes."

Eve rolled her eyes. "Don't you dare; you know you are our designated driver."

"You mean your designated driver," Carina blurted out. "Look Eve it took us almost an hour to drive here and I want to enjoy myself too," she paused. "So don't get mad and want to leave. You know who I mean."

Distracted with her thoughts, Eve stared off into the distance. She looked completely lost.

Thoughtfully Carina's eyes glittered with concern. "Evie please don't worry about that lizard Izard Moulard showing up. I don't think a rat like him will ever show his face again," she said caringly. "If that old snake ever shows his face I'll show him what I've got waiting for him in my purse."

Eve shuddered at Izard's name. She stared back at her best friend and wished she'd shut up. Carina was right Izard was a lizard and a snake. Too bad she hadn't figured that one out in advance.

It had been two years, but the memory of that night would forever be etched in her mind. That night there had been a party at an old mansion. Eve had done something she'd never done before, gone into an isolated part of the old mansion all alone. It was her realtor instincts that had led her to explore the old place by herself. To her shocked surprise Izard Moulard had somehow followed her into the empty room unaware to her.

The next thing Eve knew she looked up and Izard was watching her with the hooded gaze of a snake. He'd called her a stupid good for nothing whore that deserved what he was about to do. Eve remembered being pushed to the floor screaming. The next thing she remembered was the door bursting wide open and Izard Moulard being beaten and left lying sprawled out on the floor.

Carina laid her hand over her best friend's hand caringly. "I wish I could make it all better Eve."

"Don't worry," Eve stammered out, letting her thoughts come back to the present. She quickly changed the subject. "Gosh, I wish you would get a pair of contacts Carina. You're hiding that beautiful face behind a pair of old gold framed glasses," Eve said softly.

"These are new. Besides, everybody can't look like you Eve. You were born with smoldering good looks. You're so lucky your father was handsomely attractive. I wonder which side of his family he got it from. Was it the Mexicans, the African Americans or the Asians?"

"Dad always said it was a combination of his mixed heritage," Eve said smiling softly. Her deep green eyes were courtesy of her mother's French and Creole ancestry.

Eve turned her attention to Carina's face and studied her. She was tall, rail thin, and gorgeous. Her hazel green eyes with flecks of gold running through them could melt a man's heart. "Well baby girl, speaking of mixed heritage beauty, you didn't do too badly in that department yourself. That rich pale caramel skin color of yours was on the envy list of every girl we went to school with."

Carina rolled her eyes. "Yeah right."

"No really Eve shrugged. "Do you remember that girl in high school, Patricia Whittington? She spent a fortune on tanning booths trying to get your coloring."

The two friends laughed remembering.

Carina's glasses gleamed in the car's light.

"God Carina if you only had contacts," Eve shook her head. "You'd get a man to marry you in a heartbeat with one of those come hither looks of yours," she shrugged. "If you had contacts they would just add icing on the cake."

"I thought you said these glasses were more flattering on me?"

Eve shrugged. "Oh! No what I said was that pair of glasses only looked good on Sara Palin, but they look fantastic on you."

"That was a compliment, right?"

"My very best!" Eve said. "Come on Carina, let's get out of the car."

"Thanks," Carina's voice was muffled as she closed the car door behind her. She played with her hair. "You can be nice sometimes. Now stop worrying. I promise I'm going to have a great adventure tonight."

"Now I'm worrying. I never said I wanted you to have an adventure. I said be nicer to Grant Godeau tonight. I think he really likes you. The guy just needs more encouragement from you," Eve replied.

Carina smothered a yarn. "Yeah sure I'll be nice to boring old Grant Godeau. Did you know I've been very patient with that man? In just the last two weeks we've been on the phone at least six times trying to set up a lunch date and we haven't decided on a restaurant yet?"

Eve grinned amused. "Oh and I'm sure you were keen on rearranging your work schedule to lunch. Am I right?"

"Well maybe I did have a couple of meetings that I just couldn't get out of," Carina said.

"Apparently you couldn't," Eve said, checking her lipstick. "Look Carina, I know you are interested in getting married someday. A guy like Grant is perfect for you. Yes, he's a couple of years older than you. But the guy has his own wealth, even without the business he has with his cousins. Grant owns several exclusive office parks. Plus, he owns the Godeau building in downtown Oakland California. He has polished manners, impeccable lineage, and he has an Ivy League education. What more could you ask for in a husband?"

"An outgoing personality, for a start," Carina said feeling like a noose was tightening around her neck. "Besides once Hawke shows up he'll be the life of the party."

Carina's chattering started getting on Eve's nerves. She stopped abruptly.

"Stay away from Hawke Deville!" Eve commanded.

The moment was awkward.

Carina stood for a moment and stared at her friend, stunned speechless.

"I'm sorry I yelled Carina, what I meant…" All at once she got an inspiration and lied. "He's hiding something. Most people like Hawke Deville are always hiding something."

"But Hawke has always been a good friend to us both. Remember you said yourself. I don't understand it Eve. For the last few months you've done nothing but bad mouth Hawke. You said he was a good guy."

Eve shrugged and kept walking.

"Gosh Evie you so dislike Hawke now. Why?"

Eve sighed softly. She thought for a moment. She didn't want to upset her friend. "Yes I did say that Hawke was a good person, but that was a long time ago. I have my reasons for wanting you to stay away from him. I just think that guys like Hawke Deville don't want but one thing from a woman. And once she gives it up. He doesn't see her as anything but a whore or a slut."

They continued walking in silence.

Carina looked up at her friend thoughtfully as she played with her hair.

All at once Eve reached out her hand tenderly and pushed back a loose strand of hair. "God's sake Carina, don't go messing with your hair. It looks fabulous, as long as you don't start playing in it."

Carina swallowed hard. "Evie why do you always treat me like a kid? I only play with my hair when I get bored."

Eve chuckled softly and glanced at her friend. "I don't mean any harm pumpkin. I guess it's' that elder part of me that makes me want to protect you. For some reason I always feel protective of you. You're the baby sister I never had."

Carina smiled back. Eve always did know what to say to calm her. "Okay, big sis, you know I can never stay mad at you for long."

"Come on let's go inside. And don't get bored. Help me find my next client with potential," she said excitedly. "Oh and make sure he has a big one."

"Shhhhh Evie! God I swear sometimes you say the word *client* like you're a prostitute, or something."

"What? You know I meant a fat bank roll," Eve smiled softly with an intrigued glint in her eye. "Besides, if I was a call girl, I'd be the highest paid and yummiest call girl around. Then I'd get myself one of those *Nicole Anna* girl boob jobs," she laughed softly.

"Her name was Anna Nicole," Carina said straightening her glasses.

"Whatever. Come on Carina let's go inside. I need to find my next John, I mean client."

Chapter 2

PARTY HEARTY WHO SAYS WE WERE TARDY

The bright lights on the front porch of the old mansion beamed across the grand front door. Loud music echoed as the two friends crossed the threshold.

Carina smiled gingerly at the host as they entered.

Xavier Newhouse's expressive brown eyes smiled back. He was a local kid that had made good. He was a businessman, a former jock and a self-proclaimed gift to all women.

He reached out and pulled Carina into an embrace like the sister he'd always wanted. "Hey there Miss Cutie, so glad you could make it, oh and your best friend Evie too."

Eve looked up at the tall man standing in front of her. His jet black curly hair shone against the light. His dark eyes surveyed her in a way that put her on edge.

"Well, well, well, Miss Eve you are on my territory now. Want to pay your toll fees now or later?"

Eve frowned. "Screw you Xavier, and don't call me Evie."

"I've been trying to screw you but you just won't let me," Xavier chuckled.

More people pushed through the front entrance.

Xavier's tone changed. "Guess what? I've got four rooms set up for your dancing pleasure. There are a few folks here from our old high school."

"Really," Carina's gray eyes danced excitedly. "Who?"

"Nicholas La Cour and Quinn Rolandis, you remember them," Xavier replied.

Eve's mouth dropped opened. "Really? I had home room class with both of those guys. They were a lot of fun."

"Nicholas and Quinn were way older than me," Carina said. "But I was good friends with Nicholas' sister, Lacey La Cour. Is she here?"

Xavier shook his head. Carina was like a little sister to him. "Sorry sweetness, I haven't seen Lacey or that big mouth friend of hers Maëlle Mallard," he smiled softly. "Speaking of big mouth friends, Evie, that red lipstick really looks sexy good on you tonight."

Eve's lips curled up into a devilish smile. She flung back her long wavy jet black hair. "Why thank you Xavier," she cooed. "Now what about that tall guy Kienan Egan, he was good friends with Nicholas and Quinn, is he here?"

Xavier lifted a brow. "I think I saw him come in," he hesitated. "Is that what you like Eve, tall geeky guys. What about us solid rock hard jock looking guys? You know jocks are known to be non-stop grinding machines. We can go all night if a woman needs us too."

Eve feigned innocence and leaned in close and cupped his face. "So Xavier, my red lipstick is really turning you on huh?" She leaned in close and kissed him hard on the lips.

The kiss broke out of control. Xavier groaned and tilted his head devouring Eve's lips.

Eve took a step back and pushed out of his embrace. "My luscious red lips are as delicious as a red velvet cupcake, aren't they Xavier?"

"Yes indeed," Xavier said grinning wide.

Eve's face glowed with mischief as she tore herself away from him and ran her finger down his lips and under his chin, she licked her lips and cooed softly in a smoky sexy voice. "Well then Xavier darling, when is big daddy going to put a ring on it?

"What?" Xavier asked like a quiet marriage scared man. Embarrassment and remorse flooded him. He took a step back.

Eve closed in for the kill and slowly caressed her fingers down his chest. "Wow Xavier, who knew you were husband material."

"Marriage?" Xavier froze.

"Why yes of course, Xavier darling," Eve whispered hoarsely. "What did you think I was after, your body?"

Someone muffled a laugh.

Xavier made a face at Eve and then quickly put some distance between them.

"Great to see you Eve," a woman's shrill raucous voice sang out. "By the way I like the way you handled Xavier."

"Kitty Kennard, it's wonderful to see you again!" Eve exclaimed.

Kitty, a pretty, petite almost fifty-something with a wavy cap of ginger brown hair cut fashionable to frame her face. Kitty was the editor, publisher, and co-proprietor *of Talk is Cheap, Events, Announcements and Other Gossiping News.* It was a local gossip column and website. They were famous for knowing the goings on of local people to know. They knew if you were in or out or going up or down in the social scene in the South Bay area. Better known at the Silicon Valley or Geek Nation, as many locals joked.

Kitty giggled. "Same here, so where is baby sister?"

"I'm right behind you Kitty and you know I was hoping we'd see you tonight," Carina said. "Have you got any hot gossip?"

"God you know I do, are you two all ears?" Kitty asked.

"We are. Start talking, and ladies move in close," Eve murmured.

Kitty giggled. "Well Charlene Baptiste is screwing Jacob Whitefield."

"Everybody knows that," Carina shrugged.

"Yeah but Jacob's wife caught them screwing in her bed, and instead of throwing Charlene out on her arse She climbed in bed and joined them. She said seeing the two of them together made her horny again for the first time in years."

"What?" Eve and Carina said simultaneously.

"Yes and his wife had nerve to tell Charlene that Jacob was so boring in bed. She stopped having sex with him. She was glad he'd started having an affair with her just so that she could watch them. That woman is a total freak."

"You know Kitty it always amazes me how you know so much dirt on people."

Kitty smiled and nodded. "Yes it's a gift I have, folks like to tell me things, and I let them do the talking. Plus, I'm a good observer."

"Eve!" Suddenly Xavier's voice sliced the air. "Sorry to interrupt ladies," he said. "Oh Eve, can I talk with you about something private?"

Eve shook her head. "Not now, I'm in the middle of a conversation here."

"Later then?" Xavier asked. "And don't forget to save me a dance."

"Sure, later," Eve mumbled.

The three friends watched as Xavier moved away.

Kitty shook her head disapprovingly. "You should have said no Eve."

Eve and Carina looked at Kitty with disbelief.

"Eve shouldn't talk with Xavier, huh?" Carina said. "I get it because you think he's a player?"

Eve scowled. "Wait a minute you two. I'm the one who gets to decide who Eve talks to."

"Hang on a minute Eve. We should find out what Kitty knows," Carina said with deep concern. "Okay Kitty what do you know? Spill it."

Kitty's eyes grew as wide as saucers. "Just be careful Eve, Xavier can be possessive and old fashioned in his dealings with women. I've heard he believes it's okay to hit a woman to keep her in line."

"Oh really," Eve said in disbelief.

"The bastard," Carina murmured.

Kitty sighed heavily. "Let me give you a word of advice. You two ladies should always remember Prince Charming only exists in fairy tales. And most of all remember what is walking around today among us disguised as men, are really devils…All devils every last one of them. Oh except for the ones that are just plain dogs."

"Ah, you know Kitty it was great talking to you. But Carina and I need to talk to someone. Good bye," Eve said hastily grabbing Carina's arm and pulling her out of ear shot.

"Eve, we don't have anyone to meet."

"Shhhhh Carina, don't let Kitty know that. That old bird gets loonier every day," Eve shrugged. "Come on there's got to be intelligent life at this party somewhere."

Chapter 3

Beware of the Mayan Clark Kent, Pink Cats, and Get away from the bar...

A half hour later the throngs of people seemed to multiply. The place started to smell of cigarette smoke.

Carina and Eve stood by the hostess bar set up in the formal dining room and studied the people as they sipped their drinks.

Carina could not help but notice the small petite woman of mixed race, who sat at the bar. She had good bone structure but she had to be at least forty, judging by the crow's feet at the corner of her eyes. Her hair was a bronze shade of blond, and she wore a deep red short dress.

"Who are you staring at?" Eve asked and followed her best friend's gaze.

The two friends watched as a man walked over and sat right next to the woman, in the red dress at the bar. He openly gazed at her with great interest. The man looked like a handsome Mayan Clark Kent.

The man pushed back his glasses to get a better look at the woman.

The woman in the provocative dress shifted and uncrossed her legs. Her hands slid gracefully inside her thigh. The invitation wasn't lost on the man.

"Wow, that's an unlikely pair," Carina finally said. "Isn't he someone we know?"

All at once it hit her. The Mayan Clark Kent was Quinn Rolandis. She had gone to school with him. He still looked the same.

Carina tilted her head to the side. "Is that Quinn Rolandis, Eve?"

Eve sipped her drink. "Yeah, it sure is!"

"Hi Carina, Hi Eve," Quinn said watching them checking him out. He looked back at them with naked lust.

Quinn Rolandis stood up and pulled the woman in the red dress close to him. He nuzzled her neck. It was obvious he felt the need to put on a display.

She scolded him lightly giggling softly. "Oh Quinn you are such a bad boy."

Quinn reached out and cupped the woman's buttocks. The woman moaned.

"God Quinn, why don't you get a room?" Eve said.

"Quinn, ask her." The woman in the red dress giggled.

Quinn's eyes lit up with sensual fire. His voice chuckled raucously. "Say Eve, my girlfriend wants to know if you're up for a threesome. She said the pleasure would be all hers if you're interested."

Eve's brow rose with a flare of anger. "Why you little horny heathen bitch, I ought to kick your ass for that remark," Eve scoffed.

Quinn Rolandis chuckled rich and throaty. He closed the distance between him and Eve. He reached out his finger and ran it gently down Eve's face. He whispered. "Eve…Eve…Eve darling, you remember how gentle I can be. Don't fight over me. There is plenty of Quinn to go around. He chuckled softly. Besides, while I'm touching her, I'll only be thinking of you."

"Quinn you're a rat bastard and no I don't remember how gentle you can be. Because I never let you and your ratty paws touch me," Eve hissed slapping his hand away.

"Eve do you want me to go call Xavier or someone," Carina nervously asked.

Quinn took a step back nervously and pushed back his glasses. His manners held a pleading stance. "Relax Carina. I didn't mean any harm."

He turned back and looked at Eve. "Look Eve, Please accept my deepest apologizes. I'm sorry about that," his expression was appealing. "You can't blame a horny guy that finds you very attractive, for trying."

Eve made a grunting noise. "I see you're still a gentleman asshole Quinn," she said pulling on Carina's arm as they walked away.

A few minutes later Carina pushed open the door to the great room. "Xavier must have invited over three hundred people here tonight."

"Yes it looks like he did."

Carina and Evie slowly made their way down the corridor. Carina said, "Eve do you think Hawke is here?"

"God I hope not! Hawke Deville has major ego problems just like Quinn Rolandis. Besides the way Hawke pops in and out of our lives is like he's hiding something. Ever since when I was sixteen…." Eve hesitated and realized she was bringing up the past. The past she'd much preferred to stay hidden. "Anyway I really don't want to be bothered with him tonight."

"Eve, you do remember Hawke was sent to some kind of boarding school. Right after that night the two of you got caught having sex together."

Eve abruptly stopped walking and turned to her friend. Her signature smile disappeared. "I don't want to talk about that Carina. Not tonight or ever."

"Sorry Eve. But anyway, I heard Hawke has moved back. In fact, I heard he's been living here for well over a year somewhere."

Eve pretended to ignore Carina. But she heard every word she said. She continued walking. Carina followed close behind. The archway of the great room loomed in front of them. They entered.

Carina sighed heavily and pulled out her cell phone. Evie was starting to really get on her nerves. The light was blinking on her cell phone. She pushed the button. The caller ID said it was from Grant Godeau. She smiled seeing his name. Memories invaded her mind. She thought about the last time they'd been together. She thought about him a lot more than she let Eve know she did. She pressed the button and put the phone to her ear.

"Hello Grant, where are you? We're in the great room," Carina yelled into the phone.

A familiar laugh sounded behind her. "Well if you two aren't the hardest ladies to find in a house full of people."

Carina recognized the rich resonant voice of Grant Godeau immediately. Her body tingled at the sound of his voice. She turned around immediately and looked up at him. She played with her hair.

"Carina stop playing with your hair," Eve whispered.

Grant Godeau stood over six feet tall. His olive complexion and dark hair made him the stuff of what movie legends were made of. He wore black. Black leather jacket, black jeans and a v-neck black sweater. He held a drink in one hand and smiled revealing a dazzling smile.

"Hi Grant, you look great as usual," Carina said staring at him thought the lingering fog of her mind.

Grant gazed back at her. His gaze quickly took in her face and then lingered on his lips before he pulled her into his embrace.

"God, you two are hopeless," Eve said lifting her wine glass and moving a short distance away.

Carina pulled out of the embrace. Her heart quickened a beat as she stared back at his handsome face and attractive grey eyes.

Distracted by the way the light hit her hair, a devilish smile curled on his lips. "I'm sorry I've been so busy lately."

Relief flooded Carina. "I thought you didn't want to go out with me," she said linking arms with him.

"I'd be crazy if I didn't," he smiled admiring the glint in her eyes.

"The noise level in this place is getting out of hand. Looks like folks are starting to make this room a dance floor." Carina said. "I almost can't hear you."

Grant cleared his throat. "Come have a dance with me, Carina."

Carina quickly looked around for her best friend. "Eve, you don't have a dance partner."

Eve rolled her eyes in annoyance. "Go on kid and enjoy yourself on the dance floor. Don't worry about me. I heard there was some jazz playing out on the patio," she grinned. "I'm going to go check out the rest of the party."

Eve turned and headed for the door. Just as she walked through she collided with a man. She reached her hand out to steady herself. Her eyes stared up into the face of a man that looked as handsome as an angel or a prince. She loved the way his soft mustache was lined above his lip. And the way his chiseled beard gave him a commanding presence. The man had to be over six feet tall she guessed.

"You should watch where you are going," Eve said trying to pull off a dignified act of pretending she didn't notice how handsome the man was. She pushed past him and kept walking.

ஐஐஐ

A few minutes later, with a fresh drink in hand. Eve walked across into the marble patio. Her tall patent leather pumps clicked softly on the gleaming marble floor. Live jazz music filled the air. The music drew her closer into the room.

Eve felt her head sway a little and her eyelids droop. She tried to count how many drinks she had had. All at once her feet hurt. She felt like she was losing her balance.

"Young lady you need to sit down. Come on let me help you to the table," a woman's smooth voice said.

The stranger led Eve to a table in a corner. "There now," she said softly. "It's a good thing they put a pitcher of water on every table. Here you have a drink," the woman smiled pouring Eve a glass of water.

The water felt good going down Eve thought as she took another gulp of water and looked back at the woman. The woman had a kindly face. Her eyes glistened. She looked familiar, Eve thought.

"Thank you," Eve smiled. "I guess I was just a little parched."

"Or you had too much to drink," the woman's soft blue eyes sparkled. "Hi I'm Glenda D'Goodwrench-Jackson, of North Oakland California."

"Hi Glenda, I'm Eve, nice to meet you."

"Same here darling," Glenda replied.

Eve chuckled softly. "You know for a moment your name almost sounded like Glenda the Good Witch of North Oakland. You know like in the kid's movie."

Glenda's face didn't move a muscle.

Eve chuckled louder. "You should see the expression on your face. What? You don't believe in that hocus pocus nonsense do you?"

"I believe ladies should not stand too close to the bar for too long," Glenda laughed out. "Anyway child you know ancient ways of old can exist even on Telegraph Avenue in Oakland California, if you know where to look."

In a lighting motion Glenda waved a hand with a large ruby red ring on it. Instantly a black cat materialized out of thin air and sat in the middle of the table.

Eve stared back at the cat. She watched it as it changed colors right before her eyes. First the cat's color was a black. Then it turned to a blue green before changing to a deep purple. When Eve looked again the cat was a pretty pink.

The cat opened its mouth and yawned and then changed to snow white. It looked back at Eve, purred loudly, and then smiled and with a springy step bounced off the table.

Eve was speechless. Her face was transfixed on Glenda's.

"I think pinky likes you," Glenda's eyes sparkled with a strange iridescent light. A slow secret smile grew on her face. "So Eve are you a virgin?"

"Excuse me?"

"No Eve, I meant a virgin in the sense that this is the first time you've seen a cat that can change colors."

"Yeah…Yeah I guess I am," Eve said watching Glenda with a keen fascination.

Glenda chuckled with amusement. "Aren't you curious about me?"

"Yeah, I guess I am. What kind of witch are you? A good witch or a bad witch?" Eve asked.

"I'm not a witch at all. You don't have to have power to be a witch. But I guess folks like you must think that's what I am. My mother was hoodoo high priestess from New Orleans Louisiana," she said narrowing her eyes at her. "But I'm not a high priestess either. I come by my talents and skills naturally. I was born into them. But I guess if you had to ask was I a good witch or a bad witch, in the sense of being a good person or a bad person. I'd have to say I'm a good witch, I guess," Glenda said shaking her head. "I specialize in love potions you know."

"Love potions. Are you serious?"

"Yeah, and I'm good at it. You know I have a specialty. A drink that I designed, it has a powerful effect in awakening the desires of the heart of whoever drinks it. It's guaranteed to get you married, if that is what you desire."

Eve sighed. "Really? I have a friend who could really use it."

"Oh not yourself?"

Eve shook her head. "No, I don't believe all that hocus pocus nonsense."

Glenda looked quietly at her. "Why not?"

Eve shrugged. "Well I guess because... Look Glenda, I don't have an answer, okay."

Glenda's voice was reassuring. "Okay let's go back to talking about your friend. Does your friend have the most important elements needed for a good marriage to survive? Such as loyalty, honesty, compassion and passion for the man she wants to marry?"

Eve breathed out slowly. "I think she does. How much does something like that cost?"

Glenda glanced around making sure the coast was clear.

All at once twinkling bells carried around the wind.

Startle, Eve looked around her. "Did you hear that?"

Glenda shrugged. "Hear what?"

"It sounded like wind chimes or something."

"I didn't hear a thing," Glenda said. "Give me your hand," she said, pulling out a small bottle.

Eve gasped at the sight of the beautiful translucent crystal bottle placed in her hand. "It's lovely, look how clear the liquid is."

Eve stared closer. Something was inside the bottle. "Do I see my reflection? What is it?"

Glenda grinned. "Sometimes a person sees what they cannot live without."

Smoke swirled around the small bottle. The clear liquid quickly changed colors. Just as the cat had done earlier, the clear liquid slowly turned pink. The bottle was cold to the touch.

Eve could feel something strange happen. "Glenda, you know how I said I didn't believe in *hocus pocus* earlier?"

"Yes."

"Does that cloud of smoke say anything about me?" She looked closer at the small bottle in her hand. The smoke clouded and changed. She thought she saw a face. "I mean what's happening? What is that?"

Glenda blinked as if she saw her thoughts. Slowly she glanced around again, then leaned over and whispered. "Eve I know you can be a skeptic but there's something you should know," she leaned forward and studied the smoke. "Love is in the smoke. True love, but Eve there is danger, conflict and jealousy. You will face them all before you find the man who belongs only to you," she paused. "But in the end, true love will conquer through the conflict."

"Does it say the same for my friend Carina? What does it tell for her?" Eve asked.

Glenda smiled quietly. "Make sure you put a drop of the liquid in your friend's drink and the drink of the man she wants to marry."

Glenda rose. "Now go and if for any reason you need me just go to the Bart Station off Shattuck in Berkley and call my name three times," she said walking away into the shadow. She stopped abruptly and turned and stared back at her and murmured. "Oh Eve, you must remember to first close your eyes before you say my name three times, you understand?"

Eve nodded.

"Now please go," Glenda said softly moving further into the shadows until she was well hidden.

Eve clasped the small bottle in her hand and stared hard at it. Then she placed it in her evening bag, stood and walked back the way she had come earlier.

Glenda lingered in the dark shadows and waited and watched Eve walk away. She smiled and chuckled softly. She walked back into the light. She turned around.

A gorgeous man appeared out of nowhere. He was dressed in a classic black double breasted blazer and turtleneck.

Glenda looked up at him. She saw the glitter in his dark green eyes. "You were watching. I could feel your eyes on us the whole time. Well what do you want?"

His lips curved into a devilish smile. "Let's just say humans are creatures of want."

Glenda's laughter filled the air. "There are many things in this world and most think they are human. But I will agree with you. Humans are creatures of want," she said. "Now I ask again. What is it that you want?" she asked sternly looking up at the man.

She raised an eyebrow. For once she was speechless. The smile on Glenda's face faded. She waived her hand. "No! Don't tell me. I already know."

The sardonic good looks of the man were starting to rattle her nerves. "Oh merciful heavenly father, I'm going to need patience with this one."

"I didn't know hoodoo high priestess's daughters prayed." The man said.

"I'm a good catholic daughter I am," Glenda shrugged. "Just a little twisted in my beliefs just like most of the world," she said. "You wouldn't by chance be willing to give me a name?"

The attractive man ran his fingers through his dark curly hair. His dark green eyes glistened as he shook his head.

"I thought not," Glenda said.

Chapter 4

A Brighter day...New Beginnings...

The next day, the sun shone brightly through the window. Something was interrupting Carina's peaceful dream. All at once she figured out what it was. Someone had opened the blinds to her window.

"Good morning Carina. Smell that nice hot fresh coffee? I brought you a cup," Eve's voice sparkled with sunshine. "It's a beautiful day. Come on get up and take a shower. I'm making brunch," Eve said cheerfully.

"Go away Eve, I haven't finished sleeping late," Carina yarned.

"*Okay...*If you're sure I should. But we've got company coming over in about an hour."

There was a slight hesitation as Carina pulled her pillow tighter over her head. "Tell them to go away," she hesitated. "Who is it anyway?"

"Grant is coming over this morning."

Grant?" Carina blurted in a surprised voice. "Oh my God, he can't see me like this I've got to take a shower."

Eve smiled watching Carina race for the shower. Her lips twitched. Soon she would put her plan into action.

႘႘႘

Almost an hour later, Carina helped Eve arrange the white linen table cloth and napkins. The table arrangement was impeccable. Royal Doulton cups and saucers and crystal stem-ware lent the table a classic elegance.

The brunch menu was in keeping with the season, fresh produce. Apricot topped French toast was layered in a rectangular baking dish. Fresh fruits consisting of strawberries, blue berries and sliced peaches looked appetizingly appealing in a crystal truffle dish. Eggs Benedict sat warming in a chafing dish. Honey-Lemon muffins with peach butter sat nestled in a napkin covered basket. Sausages and Bacon slices didn't get over looked along with a baking dish of country potatoes.

"Pardon me Eve but did you cook enough food this morning?" Carina jokingly asked.

"You know men can eat. I just wanted to make sure we had enough."

"Well don't worry Eve, we could feed a small Army with this faire," Carina grinned.

"Ladies, I didn't mean to interrupt your inspection. But everything smells so good. I was wondering when we could eat?"

Eve and Carina turned to see Grant Godeau standing in the doorway. His dazzling white smile was irresistible.

"Now is as good a time as any Grant," Eve said. "The plates are right behind you on that table."

ൟൟൟ

A half hour later the three of them chatted easily and enjoyed the meal.

"Everything tastes wonder," Grant said reaching and pouring more coffee. "Frankly I'm amazed. You have such great talent in the kitchen."

"So does Carina. In fact, I've taught her how to make the cranberry champagne mimosa I'm about the serve," she said rising.

"I can get that Eve. You've done so much already. That's the pitcher on the buffet table right next to the china hutch right?" Carina asked.

"No!" Eve yelled abruptly. Nervously she glanced up. "I mean yes that is the pitcher. It's just that it hasn't been enough time for the ingredients to mix completely yet."

Two pairs of eyes turned and stared.

"Good thing I'm not ready for a mimosa yet," Carina said.

"Neither am I," Grant agreed.

Flushing nervously, Eve quickly sat back down. "Ohhhh, I'm sorry Carina. I didn't mean to yell. I just wanted you and Grant to enjoy the meal first. I'll get the pitcher of mimosas later," she said clearing her throat and hoping they didn't see through her lie.

The loud bong of the front door bell suddenly rang out.

Eve shook her head. "I wonder who that could be. I wasn't expecting anyone."

"I'll get the door," Grant said. "In fact I invited a friend. I hope you don't mind?"

Carina interrupted. "No, Eve doesn't mind. She likes to entertain. Besides she cooked enough food for an army."

Quickly Grant marched to the front door.

Muffled voices could be heard from the hallway.

Grant returned to the dining room and flashed a big grin. A man followed closely behind him. "Hey Carina and Eve this is Malak," he said quickly.

"Thank you so much for inviting me Eve," Malak said..

Eve looked up her face contorted into a look of deep surprise and pain. "Oh my God! It's you!"

Carina turned her attention to stare at the man that had just entered. She didn't recognize him. But she was sure Eve had from the look of pure shock that registered on her face. Slowly she studied the man.

He was a tall man with broad shoulders. He was at least an inch taller than Grant. He had an attractive stance that few men are born with. His jet black curly hair was combed back from his face. He wore a beard and a moustache.

He gazed back at Eve with an inviting glint in his strange dark eyes. His lips cocked into a half grin. "Eve please forgive me for being a little late. I brought you a little token to show my appreciation for your inviting me over," he said letting a gold necklace dangle from his fingers. A pendant hung from the necklace.

Eve gasped. "Wow! You shouldn't have," she said closing the distance between them and letting her fingers carefully reach out to take the necklace. She marveled at it as it caught the light. "It's exquisite the diamonds are so intricately formed into the shape," she said studying the pendant."

A mysterious elegant medallion diamond pendant sparkled in the sunlight.

"My gosh I see an angel," Eve's excited voice filled the air. "But you can't tell unless you look closely. My God this is beautiful."

Carina shrugged. "Gosh Eve that looks very expensive."

"A beautiful necklace for a beautiful woman," Malak said.

Squaring her shoulders Carina turned and stared back at Malak. Strange dark eyes sparkled back at her. She was captivated by his eyes. She wondered.

Malak hummed softly as he stared back at her.

"Carina please stop giving Malak the evil eye," Eve shrugged. "This is just a beautiful friendly gift. Malak please help me put it on."

"Sure," he said turning to clasp the necklace on her neck.

"Malak you are welcome to join us," Eve said turning around and facing him. Her fingers touched the pendant at nape of her neck at the same time she stared into his strange dark eyes. She felt energy radiating from him sending an intense sensation though out her body. Suddenly an erotic image of Malak flashed in her mind. She rubbed her face. "You…You are welcome to join us," she repeated vaguely, as she stood there staring.

Time stood still.

Grant opened his mouth to say something. "Eve…." he paused. "Are you going to let Malak have a seat?"

Malak interrupted him. "Ahhhh…I see I came at the right time. Eve you've made cranberry champagne mimosas," he said spotting the pitcher.

Eve took a deep breath. The man smelled wondered. His cologne smelled woodsy. Deep layers of sandalwood and citrus tickled her nose.

Malak sat down at the table.

All at once recognition hit her. Eve's mouth dropped opened. "You!"

"Yes Eve it's me. I was wondering when you were going to recognize me."

"Hawke Deville?"

The man ran his fingers through his jet black curly hair. "No I'm Malak Deville, Hawke's cousin. You met me the other night."

Grant's face brightened with a big smile. "You two have already met? Wow that's great."

Eve sat down to compose herself. She stared back at Malak Deville intently. She remembered back to the night before and recalled the soft perfect lined mustache and chiseled beard that outlined his jaw and those strange sparkling dark eyes. It gave him a commanding presence.

Eve sat in somber reflection. "You have the Deville family resemblance," she said speaking out without realizing it. "I mean expect for the whole hair, eyes coloring," she said muttering.

Carina studied Malak intently. She crossed her arms. "I don't think so," she said her shrewd eyes narrowing. "In my opinion Hawke Deville's deep green luminous eyes makes him way more handsome than Malak. No offense Malak."

"None taken," Malak smiled.

Eve lips curled into their signature smile. "Yes, but I think Malak's eyes hold an inviting glint in the depths of their exotic darkness."

Malak smiled. "Thanks Eve, I'll take that as a compliment," he said. "Eve it looks like you could use a drink. I'll make us both one. Is it okay if I refill your teacup?"

Eve nodded in a dazed somewhat bewildered look. She felt like she was in a fog.

Malak walked over and poured from the pitcher of cranberry mimosas. He immediately put the teacup into Eve's hand.

"Please pour us one too," Grant said pointing to his tea cup.

Malak did as he was told.

Without paying attention Eve took a big gulp of her drink.

"Hmmmm this tastes real good," Carina murmured.

"It reminds me of cranberry tea," Grant interjected.

"Hmmmm, it tastes prefect," Malak said.

"Wow, will you look at! Carina exclaimed.

Her loud words jarred Eve from her fog. "What! What is it?"

Carina giggled. "My teacup is empty. Malak you must pour me some more."

Grant sympathetically nodded his head in agreement. "What did you put in this stuff Eve? It's fantastic; I'll take another cup also."

"Carina the pot of tea is right next to you," Eve replied.

Grant shook his head. "It's not tea. I'm out of your cranberry mimosas."

Eve blinked rapidly. She shook her head to clear her thoughts. She cast her eyes across the room to the table where she left the pitcher of mimosas. She looked back at Grant and Carina for help. "What? You haven't been drinking my mimosa?"

All at once Malak fixed Eve with a blank stare. "Yes we all have been drinking your mimosas. And I must say they have been quite delicious don't you agree?"

"Did I drink some too?" Eve whispered frantically.

Carina laughed. "Eve I've seen you drink worse and still act sober. What are you worrying about?"

Grant laughed. "Carina's right, Eve."

There was a moment of stunned silence.

Malak broke the ice. His eyes lit up. "Excuse me Eve but when are we going out on our first date?"

"No!" Eve's voice boomed. She stared back horrified then rose and ran across the room to the table, where the pitcher of mimosas had sat. She ran her hand across the table. Her fingers clasped around the miniature crystal jar. She stared at it and then she did something strange. She laughed out loud.

"Listen Eve I'm sorry if my asking you out offended you," Malak said defensively.

Eve laughed harder. "When I said no that wasn't what I meant."

"Good," Malak said with a cheerful tone. "Then madam get ready because I plan to woo you."

Carina grinned. "Woo hoo, let the wooing begin. This I want to see."

Eve laughed out harder.

All at once a loud, boisterous chuckle erupted from Malak.

"What joke did I miss?" Grant asked.

Eve smiled triumphantly. "Grant, you didn't miss a thing. More mimosas anyone?"

Chapter 5

Committed relationships say what.

Two weeks later, that Sunday morning. Carina watched Eve walk over to her favorite seat at the table, by the window. Beneath her smoldering good looks, her deep green eyes showed signs of tension.

"Eve don't you think it's strange that you never have a committed relationship with a guy?" Carina asked, lifting the rose pattern teapot back on to the tray. She carried the laden tray over to the table.

Eve glared back at her. Quickly she turned her attention back to the window. The view from the window looked right into her back yard. She smiled warmly. The wicker chair and love seat were a perfect combination under the big tree. It was her favorite spot in the back yard. "You know I don't think much about things like that," she said trying to change the subject. "We should have sat outside, under the tree. It looks beautiful outside."

"Don't try and change the subject with me Eve," Carina replied. "Here's your tea."

The fragrant scent of fresh brewed tea filled the air. Eve took a deep breath. "Finally you made my favorite. Orange spice tea," Eve said taking sip.

Carina smiled softly and walked back to the stove to retrieve a tray of perfectly baked scones. Her thoughts wondered back to that Sunday brunch. The minute Malak walked into the room his eyes searched out Eve. Carina was certain about two things she saw in Malak's eyes. The first was that he wanted Eve and the second was she was sure she saw a high level of admiration in his eyes for her best friend. She suspected it was something she needed to watch more closely.

Carina cleared her throat. "Guess what, I finally perfected my cinnamon raisin scone recipe. Here taste this."

"MMMMMM that's good," Eve grinned.

Carina sat down across from Eve. "Now back to what we were talking about earlier. You are afraid of being in a committed relationship and I think it goes back to the fact that your mother caught your father cheating on her with that bleached blond bimbo secretary of his."

"Why are we talking about this? I know all about my Dad and his affairs."

"Keep an open mind Eve. I'm just saying. You never gave it a thought. That's why you're afraid to let Malak woo you. It's been two weeks and you keep avoiding the man's calls. You're afraid to go out on a date with him because you're afraid he might be the one. The one you fall in love with."

Nervously Eve laughed. "Gosh, you have such crazy notions sometime Carina."

"Well, find out if my notion is crazy. Go out with Malak. Quit hiding from the man, return his phone call and go out with him."

Before Eve could respond her telephone rang.

Carina rose. "Before you get that Eve, I really need to get going. Elena Chan promised to drop by and give me a few ideas on redecorating a couple of rooms. There's really not much to clean up," she headed for the door. "Don't worry, I'll let myself out. Oh and Eve, I'll call you later."

The phone kept ringing.

She sighed heavily before rising to answer it.

"Hello."

"Eve, it's me, Malak," his voice was resonant and warm. "Please, we need to talk?"

Eve grimaced. "Okay but we haven't even had our first date yet."

Malak was silent for a moment. "That's the reason we need to talk," he hesitated for what seemed like minutes. Then his voice breathed out enthusiastically. "God, I'd love to see your beautiful face Eve."

Eve's heart began to pound at the thought of him.

"Hear me out Eve. All I'm asking is that you go out with me. Forget that wooing stuff, and that having sex stuff. We don't have to do any of that," his words tumbled out pleading. "In fact I just read this book on how to change your life and I'm afraid I don't want any more one nighters of passionate meaningless sex."

"Let me get this straight. You read a book on how to change your life and from it you decided to cut having sex out of your life?"

Malak hesitated. "Yes, unless that scares you off. All I know is that you are a perfect fit for me. But if you're not looking for a lasting relationship, I understand. I will take what I can get. If it lasts, great. If it doesn't last, then oh well. Please let me just take you out."

Eve's resolve weakened at his words. "No, that doesn't scare me off. When?"

"Tonight, tomorrow night, the next night," he replied excitedly. "Lady, you just say the word."

"Okay how about Saturday night."

Malak laughed warmly out like a strong breeze. "Great! You've just given me all the positive response I'll ever need."

Eve took a deep breath. She felt in control of her feelings. "Oh and Malak about that wooing part, I'm okay with it," she hesitated. "So where are we going?" Eve asked.

"It'll be a surprise. I'll pick you up at seven. Oh and Eve if you have something formal, like a cocktail dress, you should probably wear it?"

Chapter 6

Eve a damsel in a black dress...

That Saturday, promptly at seven, Eve opened her front door.

Immediately Malak raised an eyebrow. "Damn, you look beautiful in that gown."

Eve looked delicious in a black sequined shimmering, slinky, curve hugging, spaghetti strap gown.

She smiled back at Malak. "Thank you. You clean up well too. Boy am I loving that tuxedo on you."

"Come on Eve, our limo is waiting."

Eve smiled at the chauffeur as he opened the rear door for her.

"Exactly where are we going Malak?"

"I hope you like the San Francisco Opera Theatre," he smiled, leaned over and let his lips brush her ear. "Did I tell you, you look stunning in that gown?"

"Yes to loving the San Francisco Opera Theatre and yes you told me about my dress," she smiled.

His lips moved to her mouth. He kissed her soft and gentle and then more demanding.

His touch was electrifying.

"Sir, I thought you said no sex?"

Malak placed his hand under her chin and lifted her face to his. He smiled and then kissed her again. His mouth slid from hers and he kissed her shoulder. "I said no to sex. I said nothing about kissing."

Eve pulled back out of breath. Every minute she spent with Malak she became aware that there was something there between them. She pulled out of his embrace and adjusted her dress. Her eyes caught sight of the bottle of champagne. "Can a girl be offered a drink?"

"Sure, in fact this guy insists," he said pouring them both a glass.

Quickly Eve downed the glass of champagne and held her glass out for a refill. Tonight she was determined to numb herself with as much champagne as she could manage.

By the time the limo made it to the San Francisco Opera Theatre Eve was dazed from both the heavy kissing and the bottle of champagne.

She remembered hooking her arm around Malak as they walked into the theater.

The next thing she knew the lights went out signaling the beginning of the night's performance.

ഔഔഔ

A couple hours later, Eve couldn't suppress her enthusiasm any longer. She pulled herself to her feet clapping her hands fiercely as the climax of the performance signaled the end of the show. Throughout the performance she had marveled at how delightful the producers had created a romantic, funny and quirky opera.

Malak had studied her all night. He couldn't keep his eyes off of her. Finally, he rose to his feet and gathered up her evening bag and pashmina shawl. "Here, don't forget your things Eve," he said helping her with her shawl.

Their hands touched. His fingers gently wrapped around hers before his hand tightened around hers. He tugged her close to him. "It's been wonderful spending this evening with you.

Malak stared back at Eve. He felt an urge to kiss her. He pulled her into his arms and kissed her.

"Naughty, naughty," an old white haired lady giggled walking past them.

The couple pulled apart.

Malak felt he should say something. "Would you like to go and have a late dinner with me?"

Eve felt a thrill run down her spine. "Yes. I would love too."

They continued walking out of the theater.

A glimmer of appreciation showed in her eyes as she stared back at him. "The show was over too soon. Wasn't the singing wonderful?" Eve asked.

Malak chuckled softly and gazed back at her intently. "Yes, it was wonderful, but for me kissing you just now was my highlight of tonight's performance," he chuckled softly and knew he'd better get the conversation off of kissing. "What else did you love about the show tonight?"

"Oh, I loved everything," Eve breathed out fervently. "I just love the story of the gypsy girl Carmen, she was fabulous," her words tumbled out. "I was mesmerized by the way she taunted Joe, the young corporal, into her dangerous game. She played Joe into a fit of jealous so bad that he ended up fighting his commanding office just to have her."

Malak shook his head enjoying her enthusiasm.

"I wish I had season tickets," Eve said. "This year the programming is phenomenal."

"Yes, it is," Malak agreed. "Don't worry I'll bring you to any show you want to see. Just name the day. All I want is to be with you."

Eve floated in close beside Malak. "Well, well, well. Mister you're making it pretty hard not to like you," she smiled leaned over and kissed his cheek.

Malak moved fast and caught Eve's lips with his and pulled her close.

"What are you two doing?" Xavier Newhouse's indignant voice sliced the air.

Eve grimaced when she looked up into Xavier's expressive brown eyes.

"I'm trying to focus on kissing the girl of my dreams," Malak's voice was disarming with laughter.

Eve looked between the two men checking to see if all was good between them.

Malak smiled wide. "Hey Xavier, what are you doing here tonight?" he didn't wait for an answer. "I know a playboy like you aren't here alone tonight?"

Some of the tension smoothed out of Xavier's face. He looked as if he wasn't sure what to do. "I just came out to enjoy the opera," he cleared his throat. "I couldn't get a date tonight. Too last minute, I'm all alone."

In a show of possession Malak moved a stray strand of hair off Eve's face. He murmured under his breath and then kissed her softly on the lips.

Eve flushed warmly. She knew the show was intended for Xavier's eyes but she didn't care. Malak was making her feel desired and wanted. Nervously her fingers touched the pendant at the nape of her neck.

Xavier Newhouse watched the whole display with a keen awareness. He knew from experience how silky and soft Eve's hair was to the touch.

He frowned. "So how long have you two been seeing each other?" his voice almost strangled in his throat.

Malak ignored his question and kissed Eve affectionately a little longer.

Then he sighed heavily. "Please excuse us Xavier, but it looks like our limo is here. Eve and I really need to leave. We've got late night dinner plans."

The lack of respect Malak showed him made Xavier furious. He didn't say a word as he watched the two of them walk away. He gritted his teeth and huffed under his breath. "You'll both get yours. I'll make you both pay for this insolence."

Chapter 07
Let's make a deal...

The following Monday morning Eve woke up and looked at the clock. It was just past seven.

"Oh God, I left the television on," she moaned.

"Good morning to you too," Carina mumbled. "I turned on the television."

Eve racked her brain and remembered. "In a lot of ways it's a good thing I gave you your own key," she paused. "Now why are you here?"

"Carina smiled. "Oh get up Eve. You know I promised to drop you off at work today, remember?"

"Gosh, I forgot. I need a cup of coffee. Will you make some?"

"I made you some English breakfast tea. Don't worry it has plenty of caffeine. I've had three cups already. By the way, you got two missed calls."

With a sigh, Eve got out of bed. "Oh really? Who from?"

"One from me of course, telling you to wake up over an hour ago and the other from Xavier?"

Eve still couldn't wrap her mind around the fact that Xavier had seen her out with Malak. She shrugged and made her way to the bathroom. "I don't know why he's calling. Let me get a shower and get ready."

ಬಿಬಿಬಿ

Later that same day, Eve was just leaving work after a hectic day.

Xavier Newhouse appeared just as she walked out of the lobby of her office building.

"Eve I'm glad I caught you before you made it to your car," Xavier said in his husky voice. "

Eve stood to full height. "Oh hello Xavier," she said in her perky voice.

"I called your house, and left you a message. You didn't call me back," he smiled. "You look hungry how about we catch a bite to eat and talk?"

Eve didn't answer. Her mind raced.

"I just want to talk," Xavier pleaded.

Finally, Eve nodded. "My car…I got a ride in to work from Carina and I was supposed to call her if I needed a ride home."

"Then everything works out. I can give you a lift home after we eat."

৪৩৪৩৪৩

An hour later, their waiter cleared their table. Eve and Xavier spoke very little over dinner.

Now that she was good and full. Eve was ready to go home. She didn't want to appear rude and quickly thought of something to say. "Carina tells me Grant is treating you to the big boxing match in Las Vegas this Saturday."

A frown crossed his brow. "Yes, Grant was really grateful that I helped him earn the Global Technologies Account."

"Xavier you don't look excited. I hear Grant's pretty excited about the trip. You both should have a good time in Vegas."

"Thinking about the trip is what made me sad. I just realized that it's interfering with my plans?"

"What?"

He smiled. "In case you were wondering. The reason why I asked you out to dinner was to talk to you about asking you out on a date," he said sipping his wine slowly. "When I saw you coming out of your office building at work, all I could think of was I just wanted to have dinner with you. And to confess to you that I want you to take me seriously. I'm willing to start slow to take this friendship to higher ground. I'll do whatever it takes to have a relationship with you again."

She glared back at him thunderstruck. "A relationship with me again?" she repeated. "We haven't been in a relationship since college and even that was one sided."

Xavier rubbed his chin. "Yes, and I'm sorry about that but I'm serious this time."

Eve breathed out. "You're serious. Oh really? So right now you're asking me out on a date?"

In a split second Xavier leaned over and reached out and touched her hand. "Yes I am Eve. I just thought of something. I'm going to Vegas this weekend. Why don't you join me?"

"Join you and Grant? No way," Eve laughed out. "Look Xavier I've hooked up with Malak. We're a couple."

"Oh really?" he said sarcastically using her line. "One date maybe two does not make an exclusive couple. Have some pride about yourself Eve. Are you and Malak exclusive in his eyes Eve?"

Eve shifted uncomfortably in her chair.

"Remember men see relationships differently than women," Xavier sighed in annoyance.

Eve's brain, as usual, raced at a top notch speed. What was the good of having pride if you had no one who really loved you? And why did men always want to bring it up. She shook her head to clear her thoughts.

"You shouldn't limit your options," Xavier said defensively. "Who knows, going out on a date with me won't be such a bad thing," he said studying her. "I'll tell you what. There's a party the following Saturday after I get back from Vegas. How about we meet there? We don't have to call it a date. We'll just hang out together and see what happens. Deal?"

Eve nodded ignoring him. She crossed her arms over her chest and grew quiet.

"Eve please I know when you nod your head it means absolutely nothing. Please say you promise me Eve?"

Then something clicked in Eve's brain. She realized the event he was inviting her to was two weeks away. What did she have to lose? "Okay, I promise," she said hating herself as soon as the words left her mouth."

Chapter 8

The Pumpkin Patch anyone...

That October Saturday morning, the sky was a cloudless blue. Route 92 heading into Half Moon Bay was both picturesque and romantic.

Eve knew she should have been enjoying the ride. But she was sure it was the longest car ride of her life. She took a deep breath and pushed her encounter with Xavier the night before, to the back of her mind.

"Where are we going Malak?"

"Well since we're almost there it's no secret. The Pumpkin Patch at Half Moon Bay," he winked back at her. "Lemos Farm is my favorite spot this time of year. I figure it was a great place to talk, walk around and get in touch with our inner child."

Eve mulled over his words then smiled lightly.

"You're smiling. That's a good sign. I think we'll have a good time," Malak said.

A short time later Malak parked his grey jaguar in the old farm's parking lot. Stalks of drying corn decorated an old gate as they made their way through.

Eve enjoyed the casual country atmosphere. Dressed in a pair of curve fitting jeans, riding boots and a soft v-neck sweater with her hair swept back into a ponytail off her face, Eve looked classic sexy cool.

Malak couldn't stop the smile of pride that touched his lips. As he gazed at the pendant on Eve's neck. The sun's reflected light made it sparkle as if an Angel's light lit it from within.

"What are you smiling at?" Eve inquired.

He smiled. "Oh, I just love seeing you wearing my pendant. It looks good on you."

"Thanks, I love wearing it," she said, touching the pendant.

She relaxed and hooked her arm in Malak's as they continued walking and talking easily with each other.

ഇഇഇ

An hour later Eve was sure they'd walked every acre of the small farm.

She breathed out slowly. "This is a great place. I forgot it's getting close to Halloween. No wonder there's so many kids about," Eve said. "You were right. This is a great place to get in touch with your inner child."

Malak grinned back at her like a man who had found heaven. He grasped her hand in his and smiled. "Come on I know where we can get a slice of the best pumpkin pie in town."

To anyone walking by, the two of them looked like a couple in love, as Malak took her hand.

A few minutes later Eve tried to hide another moan of delight as she took another bite of her pumpkin pie. Malak had been right. It was the best pumpkin pie she'd ever tasted.

Eve couldn't believe she was sitting on a large bale of hay and having a wonderful time. She licked the whipped cream from her fingers and tried not to stare at Malak's plate of pie. He was eating it too slowly for her.

A faint smile touched Malak's lips. "Did you know Half Moon Bay had their first Annual Pumpkin Festival in 1971?"

"Really? I bet it wasn't a success. First annual events rarely are."

Malak scooted closer to Eve. "Believe it or not the festival drew 30,000 people and they only had one local nonprofit on hand to feed everyone. Can you imagine how long the food line must have been?"

She tried to not stare at his pie. "Wow, no I didn't know that. You seem to know a lot about this place."

Malak breathed in deeply. "Yes I guess I do. It is probably because my mom and dad brought me here every year as a child. The first time I came here I was only three years old. My mom dressed me up in a pumpkin costume. And my parents took pictures of me standing beside a pumpkin that was taller than me," he laughed. "Every time I look at the photo I can't tell which one is me."

"Now that, I wish I could see," Eve smiled. "It sounds like you have some great memories up here."

"Yes I do. This place has always held some of the best memories for me and I want it to do the same for my children," he cleared his throat. "Who knows maybe someday it will hold fond memories for your children Eve. You do want children don't you Eve. But first, I'm sure, like most women, you want the fairy tale. Marriage and then kids, right?"

Eve tried not to stare at him. She couldn't believe he'd said that to her. She'd never really allowed herself to think about having children or the m word, marriage. She exhaled slowly. She didn't believe in the fairy tales like her best friend Carina did. Men were just men as far as Eve was concerned. There were good men, bad men, handsome men and ugly men. It didn't matter to her, men were men. They always helped themselves first and were faithful to no one. Eve prided herself on thinking she thought like a man first.

Eve suddenly realized Malak's leg was touching hers.

"*Eve,*" Malak's voice was husky as he whispered her name.

"Yes," she murmured.

"Eve would you like the last bite of my pumpkin pie?"

A wide smile touched her lips. In a low sexy drawl, she whispered. "Yes, I would love the last bite of your pie, Malak?"

Eve shifted and opened her mouth.

He placed the last bite on her tongue.

She stared at him the whole time.

All at once Malak's fingers reached out and touched her chin. "You've got a drop of whip cream right there."

"Thanks," she purred

At the feel of his touch a switch went off in her head. She couldn't hear a word he was saying. All she could hear was a very small voice inside her head telling her she liked him. She really liked him. In fact, it felt like something more.

"What did you say?"

Malak's voice was kind. "I ask if you wanted kids someday."

Eve was speechless. She didn't know what to say.

He cracked a smile and looked deep into her eyes. "Eve did you hear me?"

She sighed with a whisper. "I don't know, maybe."

Malak shook his head. "Eve you do know that's how the story ends. Boy meets girl, boy finds girl very attractive and then they procreate and make many beautiful babies."

She grinned. "So that's your design in hooking up with me?"

"Isn't it yours too?"

She cracked out a laugh. "I was so hoping to just have a relationship with a man with benefits. You know like having excellent sex several times a week."

All at once Malak leaned over and brushed his lips against hers. The kiss was soft and gentle. "I thought the absence of sex would make our love grow stronger."

He pulled back and stared at her.

It seemed as if it was the first time she really stared back into his eyes intently.

A strange light rose around them. Like a soft lighting rod tearing open a curtain between the real and surreal.

Malak's teeth twinkled and gleamed. There was a mythic quality about him.

The moment seemed supernatural.

Eve exhaled slowly. For the first time she became aware of strange feelings in her body. She leaned in close. She wanted Malak. Her body was aroused. Her head fell back and she opened her mouth.

Malak covered her mouth with his. The kiss went on and on. His mouth began to wander searing a hot trail down her face to her neck.

The air around them seemed mystically charged. Cool chills of sensations ran through Eve's body.

Eve moaned her voice cooed with sensual urgency. Her hands glided fleetingly over his body.

Malak could feel his body thrilled to the feel of her touch.

Soft lighting flashed again.

Malak felt the most erotic feeling in the pit of his stomach. He moaned with an amorphous sense of longing. He felt like he was unable to stop himself. He observed that a weird phenomenon was happening all around them.

Eve could feel her body responding to his. She snuggled in closer to Malak.

The strange soft Lighting flashed again.

All at once Malak shook out his thoughts and cleared his head. He lifted his mouth from hers and abruptly released her. "God I feel weird. Hmmmm I'm thirsty. It must have been all that pumpkin pie I ate earlier. It has made me thirsty," he said, taking a few steps back from her, wiping his mouth. Trying to break the spell he felt he'd been under.

Annoyed. Eve shook her head. "What's wrong Malak? Was it something I did?"

"Nope, it just that my mouth feels dry, real dry. I need a drink of water. How about you Eve, do you want me to get you a bottle of water?"

He didn't wait for her to respond. He skedaddled.

"Where are you going?" Eve's voice called after him.

"I need a nice cool drink of water," he said strutting toward the food trailer.

Eve got her bearing and walked a few steps to where a corral stood. She leaned on the railing and watched the children playing on an old stage coach.

The children's laughter filled the air. She leaned against the rail and thought about Malak. She never liked dealing with men who wanted her. She liked to always be in control.

All at once Eve's blood ran cold. She took a deep breath. Her breath caught in her throat. Her senses heighten as a strange awareness came over her. An old familiar feeling pulled at the pit in my stomach. Eve had an eerie feeling that she was being watched. The feeling wasn't scary; it was just a knowing. And the knowing came with a familiar smell from her childhood.

Suddenly Eve looked up. A woman was standing right next to her. She stood as silently as a living statue. She knew the woman hadn't been there before. The woman was as translucent as a vapor. The woman spoke words but her lips never moved.

In an eerie voice the woman said. "He plants the seeds so that your love for him will grow. For love is like magic just look around and you'll see. Life is a circle, the new becomes the old. And mysteries unfold. The old stories are true. As every generation is born, they must love and grow old. So as it was told. Adam had Eve, Boaz had Ruth. Look into your kinsmen's eyes and know the truth…"

A child screamed and Eve turned her head. Eve turned quickly to look beside her. The woman was gone.

"Eve! Eve! Eve! Look at me please," Malak tenderly said. "Now take another drink of water. Are you feeling better?"

"Yes," Eve said.

"Do you want to tell me what happened?"

"No… I mean I don't know," she said.

"Okay. I'm taking you home. You've had too much sun for one day."

Chapter 9

Ghosts, the little people and other scary things…

A week later, confusion marred Eve's face. She sat perched in her favorite chair in her kitchen by the window and reminisced about the kiss she and Malak had shared. It was hard for her to admit Malak was starting to grow on her.

She thought about his words. Impulses in her brain switched on and off. Malak reminded her of a boy a long time ago, a young boy who had made her dream about being married and wanting children. Malak stirred up wants in her she thought had long been dead.

"What do you mean you saw a ghost at Half Moon Bay?" Carina demanded. "I swear Eve I don't know what's gotten into you lately. Here let me pour you another cup of tea."

"Goodness Carina, your chamomile tastes wonderful. But I'm full. I don't want any more tea. You think you can fix everything with a cup of tea. But you can't fix this. I really did see a ghost."

"An angel, you saw an angel," Carina corrected her, turning to put the pot of tea back on the tray. She cleared her throat. "I don't care what you say Eve, it was an angel with a message for you."

Eve meet Carina's gaze. "Okay fine if you say so. I saw an angel. Now what does it mean?"

"Well the answer is simple. It's probably about your need to believe in love," Carina paused in deep thought. "That's it, the angel was telling you to believe in love again."

Eve gave her best friend an annoyed stare. "Stop that Carina. You know there's no such thing."

"Now look Eve just because a guy broke your heart a long time ago…" Carina stopped in mid-sentence and stared back at her best friend. She bit her lip.

"Look little girl we agreed!" Eve interrupted.

Carina shrugged. "Okay, I know we agreed never to talk about that particular man. But Eve that was a long time ago and well, you like Malak, I can tell."

"Look just because you drank a love…," Eve hesitated. "I mean took a ride on the love boat doesn't mean I have."

Puzzled Carina eyed her friend.

Eve breathed out slowly and picked up her empty cup. "Okay Carina, hit me with another cup of that tea, and this time put a little Jack Daniels in it. If we're going to have a conversation about love I want to be good and loaded."

"Okay, but I'll only pour you a shot of Jack Daniels if you promise to talk about what happened between you and Malak at the pumpkin patch."

"If you want me to talk about that you best fill my tea cup with Jack Daniels, forget the shot."

A few minutes later Carina returned from retrieving the bottle of Jack Daniels Eve kept down the hall in the liquor cabinet. She eased the top off and filled Eve's tea cup to the brim.

Carina refilled her tea cup and sat beside her friend.

"What, you're not having a sip of Jack? Oh well that leaves more for me," Eve said taking another sip.

It was apparent the Whiskey was making Eve feel well enough to talk.

Eve took a sip and said. "A woman who lets a man get under her skin is sure to meet her downfall. You remember my freshman year in college. I fell hard for a guy."

"Yeah, I remember you never did tell me the name of the guy that broke your heart."

Eve shrugged as if shaking off a bad vibe. "And I never will. Let's just say he wasn't the make a commitment like fall in love type."

Carina sipped her tea. "You know Eve, everyone thinks the guy that broke your heart was Xavier Newhouse. As I recall, you and he had a hot thing going on in college."

Eve took a sip from her tea cup laced with Jack Daniels. She thought back to the first time she laid eyes on Xavier. It was right after the first game of the season. He was all sweaty and dirty in his football uniform. The moment would forever be etched in her mind. "Hump that was almost eight years ago," she chuckled. "Sorry honey but Xavier was fun, a lot of fun. But if it was him, I'll never tell. Besides when did you start listening to what other people say about me?"

Carina smiled back at Eve. "Okay best friend let's change the subject. You promised to talk to me about love or rather about Malak and how he made you feel."

"Oh that," Eve said sipping her tea cup. "Well if you really must know Malak is not my type."

Carina almost choked. "Not your type? What type is he?"

"Okay yes Malak is a great guy. But I'm scared. He expects me to give him things," Eve replied. "For Christ sakes he wants me to give him things," she shook her head. "You know things."

Carina gently shook her head. "So you're telling me you're scared of the things that Malak wants you to give him? What are these things again?"

Eve sputtered out. "Things, little people, you know children."

Carina chuckled softly. "Oh yeah, I forgot you are scared of men who bring up that topic. Really Eve."

"Well Carina you know I'm not ready for children."

Carina smiled and patted her best friend's hand. "Eve you're never ready for children. Like marriage, you just jump in and make the best of things."

"I'm not jumping into anything with a man who wants children in fact. I'm too busy to see Malak again, ever. I've got places to see and things to do."

"Like what?" Carina asked.

Eve annoyingly shrugged. "Don't worry about it. I have lots to keep me busy."

"Yeah like what for instance," Carina egged her on.

"Like, I have tickets for that play at the San Jose Repertory Theater. And then there's that fund raiser at the Tech Museum," she said abruptly. Then hesitated and thought about what she was saying. It wasn't that she didn't trust her best friend but she knew the least Carina knew about her social calendar the better.

"Oh don't you worry I'm not telling you my social calendar little girl. I don't need you blabbing to Malak about what I'm doing or who I'm doing it with. I won't have time to think about Malak Deville."

"Eve, this isn't one of those times you run off and hide and ignore everything happening around you, is it?"

"What? Eve Chastity Lafoy doesn't run and hide from anyone," she sputtered out. "Really Carina, I don't have the faintest idea about what you are talking about," she said rising from her favorite chair.

Walking to the doorway she paused abruptly with her thoughts. She turned around. "Hey brat, I'm calling a truce."

Carina looked up at her friend and giggled. "So do you want to go do some shopping?"

"Sure, especially for shoes."

Chapter 10
The tuff go shopping...

After three hours, Eve was amazed at how much she had managed to buy. The shopping spree to the Great Mall in Milpitas, California, was supposed to take her mind off of Malak. Instead she found herself comparing most of the men that made eye contact with her to him.

Carina tugged along behind her. "Hold on a minute Eve. There is a watch I've wanted to buy in that store. Come on let's go in."

"Oh no Carina, my feet are tired."

"I'll only be a minute, I promise. Come on Eve let's go in and look around."

Eve glanced around. "Tell you what I'll wait for you on that bench right over there," she pointed and didn't wait for Carina to respond.

Eve hurried and sat down on a bench. Out of the corner of her eye she thought she spotted a man staring from a distance. The man looked normal. He seemed to be staring at her like she had just walked off the cover of *Sports Illustrated*. She smiled. She still had it.

She looked again. The man was still looking at her. In fact she thought he stared straight through her, as if he was staring at another reality.

Slowly the man moved in closer. Her eyes focused. The man was grey haired and medium height. His skin was pale. Eve wondered how she missed this. She chalked it up to needing her eyes checked.

The old man had the strangest blue eyes Eve had ever seen.

"Do you believe in love?" the old man asked.

Eve was startled by what the old man asked. She remembered reading from the bible about strangers being angels in disguise.

"Yes," she nervously stuttered out.

"A woman like you should be with the man that loves only her. I believe you have a party to attend tonight" he said.

She shrilled out. "What? How did you know about that?" she was startled by her own voice.

The old man's soft blue eyes twinkled mysteriously. "You can keep secrets from your best friend. But in your heart you know what you must do."

She clasped her hand over her mouth.

"Love is like magic. Don't forget it Eve. The man who loves you has eyes only for you. If you don't hurry, you'll be late for your party tonight."

"What did you say? You know my name?" Disoriented she turned to looked up at the old man. Like a cloud of dust that was never there. Instantly he was gone.

Eve's thoughts raced. The old man had mentioned the party tonight. Even she hadn't made up her mind she was going to the party.

"Eve...Eve Lafoy."

Startled Eve nearly jumped out of her skin.

"Eve you look like you've seen a ghost. Have you heard the latest gossip?"

"Kitty Kennard where did you come from?"

Kitty's shrilled voice giggled. "This is a mall, ain't it? And I'm a woman, ain't I. Therefore, I was born with an itch to shop."

Eve rubbed her brow getting control of her senses. She could feel her one bad nerve being rubbed raw by Kitty's voice. "Okay what gossip are you spreading now?"

"Well I guess you haven't heard," Kitty said with eager eyes. "Janeshia James and Walker Perrault are engaged to be married?"

"She's marrying that geek?"

Kitty nodded. "Yep, Janeshia never was into players, she always loved her some Geeks."

Eve breathed out in disbelief. The air around her seemed dry and stale. Fatigue etched around her face.

Reluctantly Kitty reached out and touched her arm. "Eve are you okay?"

Yeah, everything is fine Kitty," Eve said. "I'm just a little tired."

Eve rubbed her face again. "Say Kitty, would you do me a big favor and go in that store there and tell Carina to hurry up?"

"Sure I can do that," Kitty said standing up. "I'll be back with her in a minute."

Eve turned her head and smiled contently. She sighed and gazed straight ahead. She had the perfect solution. She needed a rest from all the well-meaning caring people in her life. A much needed rest, dancing the night away.

Chapter 11

Black Cadillac, selfish hearts & a whore's warning...

Later that same night, the party was in full swing when Eve arrived. She pulled her sleek black Cadillac sports sedan into the porticoes entrance of the mansion. A valet quickly opened her car door.

Eve strolled through the front door. She wore a black dress that plunged waist deep into a V-shape at the back.

"Thank God. I was wondering if you were coming," Xavier said kissing her hand. "No one can wear a black backless dress like you can Eve.

The party was given by a good friend of Xavier. He had spared no expense. From the appearance, every detail was held to a grand scale. She saw more ice sculptures then she could count.

"Let me get you a cocktail Eve," Xavier said. "They have a new mix master here that makes some of the most exciting drinks I've ever tasted," he said leading her to an open bar. "Here Eve try this drink."

Eve took the drink it was a strange golden color.

"It's the most stimulating…I mean thrust quenching drink ever," he said. "Eve, let's wrap our arms like they do in the movies. I remembered you always loved to do that," his eyes pleaded.

Eve's fingers tighten around her glass. "Sure."

Eagerly Xavier watched her intently as she took a drink.

"MMMMMMM," she said taking another sip. It tasted like heaven. "It tastes good. What is it?"

Xavier's eyes lit up with a strangely mad gaze. "It's a passion fruit martini."

"Don't you mean a martini?"

"Nope that's why they call the guy the new mix master, he puts his own name spins on the drinks he creates," he said with a pleased expression on his face. "My God, I'm glad you came tonight Eve. You don't know how happy this makes me. I know you can't wait to get to the dance floor, but first there is a friend I want you to meet. He's been looking for a house and I told him all about you and your real estate business."

"Wow that was very kind of you Xavier. I really appreciate that."

"Come on he's waiting for us in the next room."

Eve sipped her drink as she followed Xavier. They entered the room and she knew immediately who the man was that they came to see. He was standing by the window with his hands in his pockets.

As they drew closer she overheard the conversation between two women. The woman with the jet black hair cut in a wedged-cut to frame her face said, "See that guy standing at the window? He's a self-made multimillionaire."

Her pale friend with the deep red hair said. "Yeah, they all are these days. He may be a self-made multimillionaire but can he multi-task. You know like in the sex department?"

The two friends laughed out loud together.

A few seconds later she stood in front of the man Xavier wanted to introduce her too.

Xavier quickly made introductions. "Rancor this is my very good friend, Eve Lafoy."

"I'm very glad to meet you at last," Rancor Rochon smiled but barely glazed at her.

"Pleased to meet you Mr. Rochon," Eve said extending her hand.

Rancor Rochon kissed her hand. "Please call me Rancor."

A surprise glimmer flickered in Eve's eyes. The man had manners. She was impressed.

"Xavier's description of you did not do you justice. You are enchanting and a very beautiful woman. Please know I am looking forward to working with you."

Rancor tilted his head. "Xavier, please give Eve and me a moment in private."

"Sure I'll be right over there if you need me."

Rancor Rochon wasn't a very handsome man. But he had a kind of presence about himself. He oozed wealth and power.

"I know that Xavier longs to have you all to himself so I will cut to the chase, as they say," Rancor Rochon said in a quiet slow voice. "There is a home I'm interested in. Its on Black Road in Los Gatos California. It sits on top of a mountain," he nodded his head. "I love mountains. The current owner is asking almost nine million dollars for it. Xavier tells me you a shrewd business woman; therefore I have a proposition for you. Get the house for me for eight million dollars and I'll still pay you the commission of six percent on the original listed price of the house," he paused. "I'm sure the owner will be happy with the deal. I hear they are having financial problems and could really use the money."

"You mean you'll pay me commission on nine million dollars?"

Rancor shook his head. "Yes Eve that is what I'm saying."

Eve swallowed hard and tried not to stare at Rancor as if he was mad. "I know that area well. I'll check the listing, locate their realtor and make the owner an offer."

"Good, it is my intent to move into the house within the next ninety days. I'll have my secretary send around a cashier check for the deposit. You can set up an escrow account with it."

"Wow! Yes, I will, right away," she said beaming. Eve could not believe her good fortune. She was so glad she'd attended the party.

"Oh Eve I'd like to have a word in private with Xavier if you don't mind, send him over please," Rancor Rochon said.

"Yes of course," she said gushing with joy. "Oh and thank you so much for the opportunity. I know this will be a successful business venture."

Rancor Rochon was silent as he watched Eve walk over and touch Xavier's shoulder, getting his attention. A happy beam radiated around her face.

Xavier quickly closed the distance. "Rancor, my main man."

"So I've made you a very happy man huh Xavier. Now you should get the girl just as you wanted. If this doesn't sway her feelings for you, I don't know what else you can do.

"I hope it will," Xavier shrugged. "Anyway you get what you want too."

"Yes now I will buy the family home right from under my ex-wife Isadora's own nose," he laughed out. "I told Isadora I'd pay her back for sleeping with my best friend."

Rancor Rochon chuckled softly.

Xavier laughed with him. "And now you and I will both have what we've always wanted Rancor."

Eve stood at the bar and waited for Xavier. She watched as he strutted back over, his eyes locking with hers. The slick handsomeness caused several women to turn and watch as he walked by.

She was grateful to him for the business he was sending her way. Traitorous thoughts crossed Eve's mind. Xavier could be a manipulative user. Eve shook out her thoughts. She was no longer the young girl who needed people to like her.

Xavier strutted over to Eve's side. Like a man on a successful mission. He just knew the night held great pleasures for him. "So Eve, did I hook you up with a great deal or what?"

A warm smile washed over Eve's face. "I owe you one Xavier, thanks for the client. My real estate business could really use the sale."

He smiled. He'd been on edge from the first moment she walked through the front door. She'd arrived wearing that clingy black dress. He wanted to remove it from the moment he saw her. He wanted to take her somewhere and make love to her. Now everything he had planned was working out. Maybe he could have what he wanted, now. He pondered.

A raw deep primitive passion clawed at him. He needed to touch her. His tone hinted he wanted to receive benefits in kind. "Yes you owe me big time," he said leaning in close.

Every nerve in his body wanted to touch her. The intensity of his desire for her was overbearing. "But for now I'll be satisfied with a thank you kiss."

Xavier leaned in close. His lips almost touched hers.

All at once Eve turned her face.

A dark frown crossed his face. "Eve I'm beginning to think you don't have human blood flowing through those veins," he shrugged. "Alright if I have to beg, sweetheart, please," Xavier said drawing her into his arms.

"Alright Xavier, maybe one kiss, but just so you know I'm only kissing you. And I mean it."

His mouth lowered to hers. The kiss was soft at first and then he pulled her close, kissing her with a pent-up urgency of months of hunger.

Eve leaned back against the bar for support.

All at once a male voice sliced the air.

"Miss…Oh Miss!"

Eve pulled out of Xavier's arms, and straightened her dress. She blinked back at the bartender. "Yes?"

"That lady over there bought you this drink," the bartender said.

"Huh? She what? What is it?"

The bartender looked nervous. "Miss I don't want to be insulting but it's called a *wet pussy.*"

Eve turned her attention to the lady that brought the drink.

The lady's eyes locked with Eve's. She raised her glass in a toast.

She breathed out a sigh of relief when she didn't recognize her. She quickly realized the woman knew Xavier. She could tell by the jealous gleam in her eyes.

"What will you have sir? The lady offered to buy you a drink as well," the bartender said.

Xavier's lips snarled as he growled out. "What I will have is someplace where the lady and I can be alone.

Annoyance swept across Eve's face. "Look Xavier I'm going…."

In a split second a commotion broke out at the end of the bar. A glass shattered.

"Xavier Newhouse?" a drunken man's snarled voice whipped the air.

The man reached out and clenched Xavier by the shoulder. "Xavier you owe me, I bet you Big Jake would lose the fight against Boss Man, in Vegas and he did. Pay up. Where's my money."

Xavier pushed the man away. "Get your drunken hands off me Humphrey Yearly. I always pay up on my bets."

While Xavier and the man exchanged verbal assaults Eve silently made a triumphant exit.

Minutes later, the valet helped Eve into her car and was about to close the door. "Miss…Your name is Eve right?"

Eve looked up. "You're the woman that brought me that drink."

"Yes I am Miss but I didn't mean you any harm. I was just trying to warn you about Xavier. He's not a good person. Some might even say he's mean, selfish and greedy."

Eve shrugged. "Why are you telling me all this?"

"Oh, I don't know. I guess because you seemed like a nice lady. A lady who deserves a good man who loves her," the woman said with deep sadness in her eyes. The woman breathed out slowly. "And because no woman deserves to be ill-treated, by a man like Xavier, even a whore like me," she paused and opened her purse. "Here, take my card. Who knows maybe one day you and I could have a little chat, talk about the details," she said closing Eve's car door.

Eve was just about to drive away. For some reason her eyes were drawn to look at the card. The name on the card read Layla Moon.

Chapter 12
Romance, Malak and the afternoon rendezvous

Three days later, Eve realized she preferred to deal with a banker. She learned how to do so from the beginning of her career in real estate. Dealing with another real estate agent and his ego was another problem.

"Look I understand," she said shifting the phone receiver in her hands.

She could sense a slight hostility in the tone of the agent on the other line. She could tell he hated to be questioned by a woman.

"Well, will you at least tell your client about the offer, please," she paused and then pleaded. "Please, I beg you. Oh thank you, thank you," she said as she hung up.

"Having a tough morning?"

Lifting her head from the papers on her desk. "Malak, it's so good to see you. What are you doing here?"

Malak's warm, appreciative gaze swept over her. His smile told her she'd been missed.

She stared back at him. She was barraged by a sea of conflicting emotions. She missed him. No one could kiss her like he could.

He laughed. "I had your secretary pencil me in as your twelve o'clock to three o'clock appointment this afternoon."

"Oh, really?"

At that moment Penny Wisdom appeared at her door. "Hi Eve, you know Carina called and made me give this guy your twelve noon appointment. I hope you don't mind."

"No, I don't mind," Eve blushed. "In fact, do me a favor Penny and pencil me out for the rest of the afternoon."

Penny smiled. "Eve I already have."

Eve rose and walked into Malak's arms. "So where would you like to go to lunch?"

"Well I have lunch set up at my place, that is, if you don't mind."

Eve exhaled slowly. "God, I thought you'd never ask."

ಶಿಶಿಶಿ

A few minutes later, Malak drove his grey jaguar up Yerba Buena Hill Road just off highway 101 heading South of San Jose. Majestic estate homes loomed on the hillside. He turned his car into a gated drive. A huge bronzed D initial sat centered in the wide gate. Malak pushed a button in his car. The gate opened and the D initial split in half. Malak drove his car down a long road.

"This isn't a home, it's an estate," Eve said with excited surprise. She was intrigued and her face showed it. She knew the area well. The homes were expensive. The impressive views of city lights and mountainous hillsides made it worth it. "Sorry if I'm being nosey but how big is this house and how many acres does this house sit on?"

Malak chuckled. "The house is a little over seven thousand square feet and it sits on ten acres."

Eve stepped through the massive wide front double doors into a tiled foyer flanked by huge column pillars that were as high as the dizzying ceilings. They led the eye to the huge opened living room window with beautiful valley views. The home was all on one level.

"Gosh this is beautiful," she said.

"Come on let me get you a drink," he took her hand and led her down the hall into the formal dining room.

Formal dinnerware was set out on the table. The table had been set for two. Wine sat chilling in a crystal container on top of a sterling silver stand. Eve knew it had to be expensive.

"Wow very impressive," she said her nostrils took in the aromas in the air. "Something smells wonderful."

Malak opened the bottle of wine and poured Eve a glass. "It's catered. I hope you like Filet Mignon."

Eve's eyes grew wide in anticipation. "It's one of my favorites."

He held her chair. "Give me a second to retrieve our lunch," Malak said leaving the room.

He returned in seconds and placed a plate in front of her. "Careful the plate is hot."

She looked back at her plate. The Filet Mignon was topped with grilled portabella mushrooms and jumbo grilled shrimp. The dish looked impressive. "God, this smells wonderful."

Over lunch they talked.

Malak's jet black mustache was soft and lined perfectly. So was the chiseled beard that outlined his jaw line and gave him a commanding presence.

Eve found herself staring back at his face. She cleared her throat and brought her thoughts back to the present.

"What about your parents?"

"Both my parents are in Goldonna Louisiana right now. They have a home here in California too. My mother spends most of her time caring for my grandmother. And well my father, well, he and I kind of don't speak."

"Why?"

"Let's just say that I kind of messed up when I was younger. I didn't live up to my father's expectations."

"I'm sorry you and your father aren't talking," Eve looked genuinely sad. She reached out and touched his hand.

Malak searched Eve's eyes. He could see she felt a sadness deep inside for him and his father's relationship. It was one of the things Malak liked most about Eve, how she always had a tender heart when it came to those she cared about. Her eyes told him she cared.

"I like it that you care about me Eve."

She pulled back her hand nervously. "Whoa, I do believe you can read minds. I better be careful or I…"

Eve hesitated and then shook her head. She studied him and nodded. "So who is Malak Deville? Is he just one of the rich Deville kids that had everything laid at their feet?"

Malak hesitated. "No, you could say my side of the family wasn't born into the Deville money."

"But you have all of this," Eve shrugged.

He smiled. "Yes, but I earned it through hard work. But for your information I did get a small loan from my Deville family, to get my business going. So maybe I have benefited from the Deville money."

"Deville Corporation was your creation, I know because I had Carina ask Grant about you. I hope you don't mind?"

He gave her a quick glance. "No, when Grant presented all of the questions Carina had, on your behalf. He told me he was doing so for Carina. Because, he loves her and would do anything for her," he faintly smiled.

Embarrassed Eve swallowed hard.

Eve grew quiet.

"Grant loves Carina. He said he fell in love with her at first sight. I understand that sometimes it can happen that way. Falling in love instantly I mean."

"That's interesting. I mean falling in love instantly, huh, you believe that?"

"Yes, I believe a man and woman can meet for the very first time and fall in love in the moment their eyes lock."

Eve shifted in her chair. She was full and relaxed. Her thoughts preyed upon her. She thought back to the *Grand Isles* annual Christmas Ball when her eyes had locked with the deep vivid green luminous eyes of Hawke Deville. She felt his eyes on her. Shimmering heat flowed through her. She looked back at Malak. His eyes were dark brown.

"Lunch was excellent," she said swallowing hard. She was still feeling the intense heat at the awareness. Malak was still staring.

She leaned back in her chair and sipped her wine. An expensive Persian rug lay beneath the table. She kicked off her shoes and ran her feet over it. It felt luxurious. She looked around and took it all in. "I just can't believe some woman hasn't snatched you up." Her voice died in her throat as her eyes glimpsed a long hallway. A mirror reflected back a black and white painting.

Malak's eyes followed her gaze. "You've noticed my favorite painting. Care to see it?"

Eve rose. "Sure."

The large framed painting sat just at the end of the hallway.

All at once Eve gasped and grew quiet.

"A penny for your thoughts," Malak said.

Eve breathed out slowly trying to catch her breath. It looked like a Silhouette of a woman and a man dancing at a formal ball. "I can't believe how beautiful and passionate it is."

Malak put his hands on her shoulder and turned her to face him. "Remember how you just asked why a woman hasn't snatched me up, Eve? Well it's because I've been waiting for the right one."

Eve felt the heat of his touch. Her eyes searched his.

His mouth lowered to hers. He kissed her softly nipping at her bottom lip.

Eve wrapped her arms around his neck, bringing his body close to hers. She could feel his body hardening against hers, his penis insistently nudge and bulged against her thigh.

Malak was ablaze with sensations. He knew Eve was opening up to him like never before. Slowly he pulled out of her embrace and looked back at her. "Eve you do know this is the doorway to the Master bedroom? Once we walk through this door there's no turning back."

Eve moved in closer and kissed him hard. "Then take the hint and take me there."

Malak groaned and swept her into his arms and carried her to the bed. He slowly lowered her beneath him.

Eve helped him peel away her clothes. Quickly their clothes joined together on the floor.

The instant they both were naked he looked back at her.

Malak grew still.

"What is it?" Eve asked.

"Nothing," Malak murmured distractedly, his eyes focused on the pendant hanging around her neck. He'd almost forgotten he gave it to her.

"I just love seeing my necklace hanging between your breasts," he smiled as his fingers gently caressed her breast.

Eve shuttered as his fingers left a hot burning trail that left her nipples erect.

"I love it too," she smiled.

"Eve you're beautiful," he whispered hoarsely. "I want you so much," he said as his hands moved down her body to the curve of her breast.

Malak's mouth captured hers. She was everything he'd ever wanted.

Eve released a deep moan of need at the feel of Malak's intimate touch. She shuddered with intense pleasure. Instantly her body trembled as she clutched tighter and tighter to him. He held her tight as they climaxed together.

Chapter 13
Selfish heart I ain't over you yet...

The next day, Eve dashed across the underground parking lot heading for the stairway leading to a restaurant.

The Left Bank Restaurant at Santana Row was known as a power lunch restaurant with its expertly prepared simple faire and lively conversations.

"Where are you Eve?" Carina yelled into the cell phone again. "You're late for lunch."

"Carina, stop yelling. I'm walking into the restaurant as we're speaking. Oh and do yourself a favor and hang up now because I'm sitting down at the table."

Carina nervously looked up at Eve as she sat down and laughed. "Oh, there you are. I was just getting a little worried. So where were you all night?"

Eve shrugged. "Didn't Penny Wisdom, my secretary, tell you I left yesterday to spend the afternoon with Malak?"

A faint smile touched Carina's lips. She nodded. "Which means things must have worked out," she said blinking rapidly with mischief in her eyes. "I take it the sex was good?"

Eve slowly glanced over her menu ignoring her friend.

"Well?" Carina asked.

"What are you ordering Carina? I think I have the Sandwich De Poulet."

Eve looked up at her friend. Carina was grinning from ear to ear. "So what are you ordering?"

"Oh Eve, stop torturing me and tell me. Was the sex good or not with Malak?"

Eve shook her head. "Oh, I thought we came to have lunch."

"From that satisfied look on your face Eve, I bet Malak really was good. You look like the cat that drank the whole bowl of milk and loved it."

Eve laughed out softly. "Malak really was great. In fact, he was all those things they write about in romance novels," she gushed. "He was the kindest, gentlest guy with the most skilled knack for making a woman…" she hesitated and exhaled softly. "Well anyway, you know what I mean."

"I knew it," Carina beamed excitedly. "You and Malak seemed so right together and just now you seemed so relaxed and happy. It made me happy for you. Finally, you are in a relationship."

"Hold on. There goes that imagination of yours," Eve replied. "Yes, I will admit you did feel we were right for each other from the start. But I don't know about that relationship thing. Let's just wait and see where this goes."

Carina nodded.

"Okay let's order." Eve suggested. "I'm starving."

A waiter took their order.

Moments later Eve stared back at her friend and noticed the content and happy expression on her face. "So how are things with you and Grant? You look happy too."

At the sound of Grant's name Carina giggled softly. Her eyes twinkled as if in a daze. She recited her words like a verse from an old Hollywood romance. "Grant and I give each other meaning. The word love is too weak a word for what Grant and I have. We don't need anyone's permission or acceptance for our love."

Eve chuckled softly and shook her head. "Dramatic, I'm impressed. But tell me, did you think that one up or did Grant?"

"Oh Grant quoted that to me one night. Or something similar. Anyway I kind of spiced it up and adlibbed the whole thing," she laughed. "Sounded pretty good huh?"

"I will say this Carina you and Grant watch way too many romantic movies."

The waiter brought their food. Eve sipped her wine and looked over the rim at Carina. "God, I don't know how I got so lucky!" she exclaimed. "And guess what Carina? I even had a couple successes at work this morning. I've had three deals that closed and they brought in more money to the firm than that one deal that fell apart that Xavier sent my way."

Carina swallowed a bite of her food. "What deal did Xavier send your way? Eve you never told me about a deal."

"Oh, it was nothing. I thought I told you. Xavier introduced me to a friend that wanted to buy a house on Black Road in Los Gatos. The guy said I would get the full six percent commission on a nine million dollars deal. But for some reason it just never happened."

Carina flinched. "And you thought Xavier's offer to help you was sincere?" Carina asked taking a sip of her wine. "Come on Eve you should know Xavier by now. He's a manipulative, selfish, conniving man. He wanted something from you."

"Carina, I think you're being perfectly silly. I'm not saying Xavier can't be all of those things," Eve replied with optimism. "But this time I think you are wrong. I didn't make the sale, therefore there is no commission. End of story."

"Hump, I guess you're right."

Carina sighed. It did matter. She couldn't shake her suspicions about Xavier. Maybe it was because of the way he looked at Eve. She caught that cold distance look in his eyes watching Eve too many times to count. Still it wasn't like Eve to not tell her things.

She shook out her thoughts and sipped her wine. She looked over the rim of her glass and choked out. "Eve don't look now, but the devil just walked through the door."

"Who?"

Carina lifted her hand over her eyes trying to hide. "Oh great, he's behind that fern right now. I pray he doesn't spot us."

"Look who's here! Eve and Carina, I'm surprised to see you!" Xavier announced.

"Oh damn!" Carina murmured.

"Hello Xavier," Eve said, as he stood by their table. "It's good to see you, I'm sure my best friend Carina feels the same," Eve said smoothing things over.

If Xavier was offended, he didn't show it. He was distracted by the way Eve had styled her hair. Her face was framed by several long wispy delicate curls of her long black hair. His fingers itched to push them out of her face.

"I saw the two of you and wanted to come over and say hello," he said fixing his gaze directly on Eve.

"Wasn't that thoughtful of you Xavier," Carina said tensely. "Well we don't want to keep you. We know you're probably in a hurry."

"I'm not in a hurry," he replied. "But I see you two are having a girl's day out. I must be spoiling your fun."

"Yes you are," Carina frowned. "But actually Eve and I are celebrating."

"Oh really? he asked not taking his eyes off of Eve. "What's the occasion? Did I miss your birthday or something special Eve?"

Eve cleared her throat. "Carina's joking. It's nothing like that. Carina and I are just celebrating my having a date with Malak."

"No I'm not joking and we are too celebrating," a smile played on Carina's lips. "We're celebrating Eve and Malak's spending a night together. The entire night together."

Immediately something dark, cold and sinister flashed briefly behind Xavier's eyes. "What!" Xavier's voice bellowed like a foghorn.

Every head in the restaurant stopped, turned and stared.

Eve shuddered. She felt for her friend. "Oh Christ."

As soon as the words were out of her mouth Carina wished she could take them back. "Oh crap I…"

Eve's thoughts raced trying to think of something. "Carina just meant that Malak and I spent a crazy night together having fun. We must have hit up every club in town."

The moment was silent and tense.

Xavier's eyes a spasm of jealously murmured low out of his throat. "Yes, one could say Malak is crazy."

"Ah…I…" Eve almost said. For some reason Eve didn't' know what to say.

"Be careful Eve. Sometimes you can be too trusting of people," Xavier warned, his voice was sharp, his gaze cold.

"You coming, Xavier? They have our table ready," A man's voice sliced the air.

"Yeah," Xavier said before taking his eyes off of Eve's face and walking away.

Eve drew in a deep breath. She was glad Xavier was gone.

"Gosh, you know for my part I always thought Xavier was strange. I think he's the one that's crazy," Carina said.

Eve nodded and sipped her wine.

"You know what Eve; I hate to say it but Xavier wants you bad. If I were you I would make sure he knows you're having sex exclusively with Malak. In fact, you should go by and see Malak tonight too," she shrugged. "Make sure Malak leaves his mark all over you. Have sex with him all night tonight, tomorrow night and every night hereafter."

Eve's fingers tightened around her wine glass. She hated to tell Carina the truth. In her haste to leave Malak's house and get to work that morning she hadn't spoken to him about making any plans to get together again. In fact, if the truth was told, she hadn't spoken with Malak all day. What had she been thinking? She and Malak really didn't have a relationship at all. All they really did was just have sex.

"Gosh, you know tonight Malak said he already had plans. He had a prior business meeting scheduled for tonight." She lied and prayed Carina couldn't see the truth.

Chapter 14
Lies, lies, and more lies...

Eve regretted she had lied to Carina. But she figured not being at home was the best way from getting caught in that lie.

The Orpheum Theatre in San Francisco California was the perfect place to hide. Crowds of people beautifully dressed filled the stairwell of the theater.

Eve wore her red A-line satin strapless cocktail dress. She accented it with a faux Black Fox trim Persian lamb jacket with crystal embellished buttons. Her long black hair was swept up into a vintage pinned up victory roll that framed her heart shaped face.

She found her seats in the balcony and breathed out slowly. She had the whole booth all to herself tonight.

She sat proudly in her seat enjoying the view from the balcony seats.

Looking down on the main floor below, her heart suddenly skipped a beat.

A tall good looking man slowly walked the orchestra pit. He was too far for her to get a good look at him. It was apparent he was tilting his head looking for someone.

Just then the lights in the theater dimmed. And the music began. Colorful costumes raced down the aisles.

Over an hour later, Eve's eyes were still focused intently on the stage in front of her. The music was intense and sent thrills down her spine.

Someone walked into her balcony. Eve was attentive to the performance on stage. She never noticed.

"I'll say the best performance of the night was my seeing you walk across the lobby in that dress. Eve you look fabulous tonight darling," a man's husky voice said. "I will say that shade of red suits you."

Eve's spine stiffened at the sound of the familiar voice. Her head turned around in shocked disbelief.

Even in the dark, Eve could feel the smile of Xavier Newhouse expressive brown eyes.

"What are you doing here Xavier?"

"It's almost intermission. You don't mind if I sit for a spell Eve?" Xavier sat next to her without waiting for her response. "I love coming here. It's my thing to do. I know you normally come here with Carina. I've seen you both before."

Eve nodded remembering. "Oh yeah, I do and normally you have a date. Who is it tonight Xavier?"

Xavier gave a snort of laughter. "It doesn't matter. You know Eve, I wish it was you. You don't know how many times I wished you took me seriously."

He gave her an irresistible smile and ran his finger lightly down her arm and leaned over and kissed her ear. "I've missed you Eve and the things we did for each other."

Eve swallowed, feeling his feverish touch. There was a time when that grin could make her drop all of her clothes.

"I can see you've missed me too Eve," Xavier murmured.

"Look Xavier I'm seeing someone else. In fact, I believe we're both seeing other people."

"That's bullshit Eve and you know it. You're here tonight all alone Eve. And it doesn't matter whom I'm seeing if you say the word it's only you and me."

"Look I'm not into you like that anymore," she hesitated. "I'm in a serious relationship."

"With whom?" Xavier gave a mirthless laugh.

Eve wanted to slap the smug look off of his face. Before she knew it she blurted out a name. "I'm seeing Malak Deville now and he wouldn't appreciate my stepping out on him."

Xavier gave a laugh again.

"Shhhhh, we're in a theater."

Xavier reached in his pocket and pulled out a small discreet pair of opera binoculars. He handed them to Eve.

"What?

"These babies will allow you to see the best performance of the night," Xavier said. "Just angle them to the right of the orchestra pit and tell me what you see."

Reluctantly Eve did as she was told.

Suddenly a chill gripped her as she watched Malak's face come into focus. He was sitting with a very attractive woman. Eve was focused on them at the right moment to see the woman and Malak engaging in a passionate kiss.

"Oh my God!" Eve whispered to herself over and over again.

Eve looked completely lost.

"Jealous are you Eve?"

"I can't believe this is happening.

Eve covered her face in her hands and took a deep breath.

"Eve you know the best way to get over a person is to go out with a new person. So how about it Eve? Why don't the two of us go out? It will make you feel better."

The moment she did Xavier closed the distance between them and pulled her into his embrace.

Eve calmed herself. "I wonder who she is."

Xavier's voice tensed. "I don't give a damn about her. I want to see you Eve, tonight," he snarled. "And if you don't want me putting your business out for everyone to hear or see. I suggest you agree to give me what I want Eve."

"What are you talking about?"

"I'm talking about us. You need to be with me."

"I'm not afraid of you Xavier."

"Nope you're probably not afraid of me and that's what I love about you Eve," he paused. "But since I knew I'd need a little help. I brought alone my little friend. Take of look at this."

Eve looked at the cell phone Xavier was holding.

Several photos flashed before her.

All at once Eve gasped out.

Xavier laughed out feeling powerful.

"Why do you think Malak pulled that being celibate stuff on you in the first place? Because he knew he was sleeping with another woman," he laughed out.

"Wait a minute, the best photos I have are of you. Look here."

Eve covered her face in her hands and took a deep breath.

Panic coursed through Eve as she stared back. She felt the blood drain from her face. "Where? When?"

"Close your mouth Eve. I'm sure you probably don't want your new boyfriend seeing this," he closed his cell phone. "Just be at my place on tomorrow night, nine o'clock sharp."

Eve opened her mouth to protest.

He didn't give Eve a change to object. He placed his finger on her lips and chuckled softly. "I'd much rather see you tonight but I don't think I can get out of my date," he paused. "Oh and Eve, you'd better be ready for me."

Eve watched his back as he walked away.

Chapter 15
I put a spell on you taste the bitterness...

Sunday morning, Eve had spent a sleepless night watching infomercials and doing a lot of thinking. She was sure running into Xavier was the end of her life. She resolved that she would stay in bed for the rest of her life rather than face the mess she had made.

All at once panic coursed through Eve as she stared back. She thought she saw a shadow in the hall. She felt the blood drain from her face. "Oh my God?"

"Close your mouth Eve. I can't believe you never use that secret passage. My God this room looks like a pig pen," Carina announced as if nothing had happened.

"You know I hate it when you do that," Eve grimaced. "You know I forget that passage is there."

"Eve what are you doing still in bed?" Carina's voice asked. "Girlfriend are you eating Ben & Jerry's?"

"I needed therapy," Eve said shaking her head. "Remind me to have you give me back my key."

Carina gave a snort. "Eve you don't mean that. One, two, three, Eve there's three empty cartons here."

"They were pint size."

Carina started picking up the room. "Okay what's wrong?"

"Nothing." Eve quietly said, propping herself up on a pillow. She reached and grabbed a magazine from the side of her bed.

"Nothing doesn't eat three cartons of Ben & Jerry's and two bags of Doritos' chips," Carina said. "Eve say something. Or should I guess that you have man trouble? Is that it. You went out with a new guy last night didn't you?"

Eve lazily flipped through her magazine and took a quick glance at her friend.

"Oh Eve I really thought you liked Malak?"

"Eve looked up doubtfully. "Give me a break Carina you know I've never been into that normal relationship thing like you."

"No Eve, that's not true," Carina said sitting down on the bed.

Eve looked at her best friend for a long time. "Carina you know what it was like for me being an only child," her emotions showed all over her face. "I was lonely until you became my best friend."

"That's why I know you so well Eve. You're scared because Malak has gotten under your skin too fast. When a man acts to quickly around you, it makes you nervous."

Eve rolled her eyes at her and tried to ignore her. She loudly flipped the pages of her magazine. "I don't know what you're talking about."

"You're afraid you will fall in love with Malak. Is that what you're afraid of?"

"Go away Carina, you don't know everything."

There was humor in Carina's eyes. "That's Saint Carina to you, my best friend forever. And yes I do know everything, especially about you," she said. "For instance I know that right now you're trying to make me mad. So I'll leave you alone, because all you really want to do right now is try and think of ways to get out of liking Malak."

"You had it right about my wanting you to leave me alone. But that other idea you have in your head is dead wrong."

Carina shrugged. "No its not."

Eve grabbed her pillow and whacked it hard. She knew she was losing the battle with Carina right now. She stared back intently. "I'm trying to read my magazine here. Why don't you go find Grant and tell him things he doesn't know, like how much you like him?"

"Because right now I'm trying to save my best friend from herself," Carina said her brows furrowing over as if she was really thinking things through. "I don't know I'm guessing on this one, that maybe you have some unfinished business with some guy that you thought might have been the one," she nodded. "Don't worry. I'm not going to guess any names. I don't want to have to lie."

Carina walked over and adjusted her friend's pillows. "You know there are really no rules on love in the universe. All things are possible. Did you know there's this witch lady or is she some kind of matchmaker lady? Anyway I forget," she shrugged. "She has this ad that promises she can help you with any relationship? Her name is Glenda something. Oh what was it?"

Eve's ears perked up. She straightened up in bed and closed the magazine.

Carina whacked her brain in deep in thought. "Oh where did I read it? Was it on the internet or was it an ad on TV?"

Eve's eyes were attentive.

In a split second Carina's face broke out in a smile. "Oh yeah her name was Glenda D'Goodwrench-Jackson. Her ad said she was one of the good witches of North Oakland California."

Eve surveyed her friend. It was uncanny how much Carina seemed to know.

In a split second revelation hit her. She now knew what she had to do. All she needed was for Carina to leave. Her thoughts formed.

"Carina shouldn't you go and check on Grant? I mean you've been over here with me for hours. Grant probably misses you. I wouldn't want Grant to feel you're neglecting him."

"Well I guess I should be going," Carina said bolting from the bed. "Oh by the way, I've already had a talk with Grant. He knows I like him a lot. In fact, I'm in love with him and guess what Eve? He says he's been in love with me all along."

"What?" Flabbergasted Eve yelled after her. "I knew that."

"Oh no you didn't, not until I just told you now." Carina said determined to have the last word as she closed the door behind her.

Chapter 16
The Shattuck Station it's in the air...

Hours later, Eve stood under the sign at the Bart Station off Shattuck in Berkley California and wracked her brain trying to remember what Glenda D'Goodwrench-Jackson had told her to say.

Slowly she walked to the escalator and stood just off to the side of it. She touched the pendant at the nape of her neck. It gave her comfort. Her eyes traveled up to the ceiling. For several seconds she stood there staring at the rotunda ceiling. At the center of it was a circle window dome that reminded her of a time machine. As it stared back at her, she felt like she was entering a time warp.

She cleared her throat. "Glenda D'Goodwrench-Jackson…Glenda D'Goodwrench-Jackson… Glenda D'Goodwrench-Jackson," she said three times.

Nothing happened.

And then she remembered and closed her eyes. She called Glenda's name again three times as her heart pounded.

At the precise moment she said Glenda's name a third time there was a rustling sound behind her. All at once there was a crack and a loud popping sound.

Immediately Eve screwed up her face at the sharp smell that whiffed the air. The smell was like nothing she ever smelled before.

"You called?" a voice to the right of her said.

"God what's that smell?"

Glenda's blue eyes sparkled. "Oh does it smell like a cheap hooker on a booty call, mixed with drunkard piss and sewer water?"

"Yes," Eve shrugged.

"Well honey that's nothing but the fragrant smell of the Berkley Bart station. If you really want to smell something, come back after the fog moves in and makes everything crisp and sharp, like rotten stinky cheese gone bad."

Eve grabbed a tissue and put it to her nose and took a couple of breathes to calm her mind.

"So what do you want to see me about?" Glenda asked.

Eve hesitated. "I think I may have screwed up the love potion you gave me and gave it to someone who I didn't mean to give it to. But that's not really why I'm here. I've got another guy trying to black mail me into having sex with him," Eve slowly told her the story about her and Xavier.

Glenda rubbed her face. "You really do badly with men don't you Eve?

Eve shook her head.

"Well Eve, your story is as old as time," she said shaking her head. "You've got two men in love with you and you don't know which one you're in love with. Your story is the stuff great soap operas are made of." Her blue eyes sparkled radiantly like a blue diamond. "Come Eve, we go now. We need to finish this conversation at my shop."

"Your shop?"

"Yes, it's just around the corner. Besides you need help dressing for your date tonight."

"What? I am dressed," Eve said. "This is what I plan to wear tonight."

Glenda shook her head looking around. She leaned in with urgency. "Now Eve darling putting on a pair of Geeky Girl reading glasses and hiding that beautiful body of yours in an oversized ugly sweat shirt isn't going to turn off a man. You've got to work with the arsenal stockpile you were born with. We've got to harness that power of yours," she said lowering her voice to a whisper. "You'll need it, there's a bad moon rising."

Chapter 17
Whips, lips, hips and other things...

Later that same night, the moon was a luminant silver glow as Eve made her way to Xavier front door.

Eve reached behind and adjusted her black lace thong before she rang the doorbell.

Music blared from the house. She was sure she heard Creedence Clearwater Revival.

"Whoa, thought it was a nightmare, low, it's all so true
They told me, don't go walkin' slow, the devil's on the loose"

Xavier Newhouse opened the front door unbuttoning his black shirt. "Baby I'm so glad you made it," he said waiving her in.

Eve walked in and swept aside her hair signaling for him to take her coat.

Xavier took her coat and let out a breath. "Damn you're dangerously delicious." He fought hard to slow down. "Do you want a glass of wine or something?"

Eve stood there in a black lace bra and thong. Her skin was perfect. She wore nothing else but thigh high leather boots. A small black leather whip was attached to her right thigh boot.

Eve took charge of the situation. Her eyes narrowed. Her voice was low like a purr. "You've got something I want. And I've got what you need," she said in a sexy drawl, letting her hands cup her breasts. "This is strictly business not pleasure," she turned and stared at him. "Do you have the fireplace going in the bedroom?" She asked.

"Yes."

"Good, then what's your pleasure? Whips, Lips, hips or fingertips?" She asked then hesitated. "Oh and I do want the negatives to my photos or all hell will break loose Xavier!"

She led the way down the corridor.

Xavier followed with a wide grin on his face.

In the bedroom Eve closed the door. She walked slowly toward him.

Xavier's heart was pounding. The moment was intense. His chest clenched. His throat was dry.

Eve walked over and touched his chest and quickly released the buttons from his shirt. "Xavier I'll take that drink now."

Quickly Xavier poured from the decanter next to the bed.

Eve intertwined her arm with his. "Let's drink like they do in the movies," she purred.

He smiled back hungrily and agreed. He thrust back his head with the heady drink just as she did.

Then without a word Eve leaned over and kissed him. His lips covered hers and coaxed them apart.

Eve eased back against the bed as her tongue crept forward searching for his. Then the kiss broke out of control.

Xavier tore his mouth from hers. His tongue traced down to the valley between her full breasts. He fought to slow down but found that he couldn't. He took one firm nipple in his mouth and sucked hard. He moaned. He felt like he was under a spell.

"God I want to be inside you Eve." He was burning with desire for this woman. His cock stained at the walls of his pants.

"Eve…Eve…Please help me take my pants off?"

He froze. He thought he heard a rumbling. He looked back at Eve. His body tensed.

A split second later Eve thought she heard the song again.

Better run through the jungle, don't look back…

The last thing Eve heard was Xavier growling. Before he fell forward on top of her and fell fast asleep.

"Xavier?"

Eve called his name again. "Xavier? Are you alright?"

"He can't harm you. He's asleep." A woman's voice sliced the air. "Just push him off of you."

Eve pushed as she was told. She looked to see where the perky high pitched voice was coming from.

A small petite woman stood at the front of the bed.

"Who…Who are you?"

"You really want to know if I'm real, don't you Eve?"

Instantly Eve scrambled to her feet. "Well yes."

"I'm not a ghost or a witch," the small framed woman said. "I'm Matilda."

"Well Matilda it's nice to meet you and I'm glad you're not a ghost or a witch. But you kind of interrupted me...I mean Xavier and I."

"He wasn't meant for you," Matilda said. "He isn't your type anymore. Besides, you just came for your photos. They're in the nightstand under the liquid decanter," she paused. "So are the negatives."

Eve walked over and opened the drawer. She grinned wide. "There it is."

She swirled around. "Why did you help me?"

"Oh, didn't I tell you? I'm Glenda D'Goodwrench-Jackson's assistant, Matilda. "Now Eve you really should be more discreet in the future. Make sure nothing like this ever happens again. Come on I'll walk you to your car," she smiled. "You must leave before Xavier wakes up and wants to finish what he started."

A few minutes later Eve stood at her car.

Matilda watched as Eve's eyes sparkled. "I don't know how to thank you Matilda," she said giving the small woman a hug.

Matilda watched as Eve drove away.

A laughing voice buzzed the air and cleared its throat. "Oh assistant of mine. Didn't you forget something?"

"Hmmmm Oh yeah, Eve, I can't stop Malak from discovering that you'd been here," Matilda yelled out as Eve's car drove away.

The chilly night air whipped.

"Oh dear me," Matilda said shaking her head. "Do you think she heard me?"

"Hump...Hump...Hump. My assistant you have much to learn," Glenda said as her eyes sparkled with a strange iridescent light. "No…No…I don't think she heard you. But she'll soon discover what she needs to know."

Matilda cleared her throat. "I just hope everything will be okay between Eve and Malak. I hope I didn't mess things up."

Glenda smiled wide. Her white teeth gleamed in the moon light. "She is still wearing the pendant Malak gave her. That is good."

Why?" Matilda asked.

"Because true love never fades and because she is protected by the angels as long as she wears the pendant. I would not fear for Eve."

"But Glenda what about your love potion," puzzled Matilda asked.

"Come along Matilda, I can't tell you everything. Wait and see what happens between the two young lovers."

Chapter 18
Tortured heart sees all...

Eve looked at the clock in her car. It was 11:30. She smiled, thinking of the peaceful sleep she was going to have that night. Now that she had her photos and the negatives.

She pulled into her garage and closed the door. She entered the house through the kitchen door and quickly turned on the lights.

Instantly lights brightened the house. She walked from the kitchen into the arched hallway.

In a split second her front doorbell was ringing.

A shiver ran down her spine as she went to the front door and looked through the peephole.

It was Malak Deville.

She opened the front door without thinking. "Malak it's late. You scared me to death."

Malak was wearing a tuxedo. He looked stunningly handsome in his tuxedo.

He stood in front of her and looked her up and down. He was so close to her she could smell his aftershave. "Great costume, I hope it was a fun party."

Eve did a double take and looked down. Her trench coat was open. Thoughts raced through her mind about the shameful performance she'd done with Xavier hours ago. Quickly she tied the belt. "I…I…" She swallowed hard.

Malak walked past her.

"Could I have a drink or something, Eve?"

"Sure, the bar is in the dining room, just follow me," she said as the heels of her boots sharply clicked out a staccato beat with each step as she walked across the parquet floor.

Slowly she retrieved a glass from china hutch. The hutch was right next to the buffet table. Her brain clicked and she stopped and stared at the buffet table remembering the pitcher of cranberry mimosas. That was the day Malak first walked into her life. She realized all Malak ever wanted to do was share her life.

Eve whirled around and faced him. "Will cognac do?"

"Yes," he nodded.

Eve poured their drinks. She handed a glass to Malak and asked. "So where are you coming from so dressed up tonight, Malak?"

Malak took his drink and walked over and sat down in a winged chair at the far end of the room. He was the picture of royalty as he dangled his glass of cognac in one hand. "Tonight I was on my way to the opera. But then I realized I'd forgotten something."

Eve gave a carefree shrug as if it was nothing. She looked up with realization that the vibe he was giving off was laced with anger.

Their eyes met. A long moment paused.

"What's on your mind Malak?"

He paused and stared back at her. "Did anyone ever tell you how nosey you can be Eve? I'm just a man with his thoughts and a wonderful glass of cognac to wrap my hand around."

"I can be nosy. But what woman can't? You didn't answer my question, so I guess I'll repeat it. What's on your mind Malak?"

He laughed and breathed out slowly. "You and I are perfect for each other Eve. Except you need to improve in the decency department. That's what I was thinking about."

He took another sip of his cognac and breathed. "Eve do you have something you want to say to me?"

Her jaw dropped. "I don't know. Do I? You are the one questioning my decency," she hesitated.

"Eve are you having an affair with Xavier?" His voice shook with emotion.

"What?" she whispered and couldn't meet his gaze. "I should be asking you that question."

Malak's jaw trembled. He was speechless. He rose and started pacing the floor.

He didn't have to answer her she could see it in his eyes. The truth was inevitable. She took a moment to compose herself. "I saw you with her the other night."

"You saw me with a woman?"

"Yes, at the opera."

"And you think I'm seeing her?" Malak shook his head. "Baby it's not what you think. That woman, we're not together. Please, I can explain."

Eve turned away, put down her drink, gripping the hutch. "You two seemed very together to me," she said quietly.

She squeezed her eyes tight. "I thought you said I meant something to you Malak was that a lie?"

Malak closed the distance between them. Then stopped abruptly and stuck his hands in his pockets. "Hold on a minute Eve I'm very flattered about everything you're saying. But you've got your facts a little mixed up," nervously he gazed back at her. "What about what I saw tonight. I saw you with Xavier.

Eve turned around and faced him. "What?"

"I saw you tonight with Xavier," he repeated.

Embarrassment showed on Eve's face.

Malak rubbed his brow. "I went to Xavier's house tonight. I saw you go to the front door. Xavier let you in. You walked inside. I stood outside the doorway and I watched him take off your coat."

She ran her hand across her mouth. She looked down at the way she was dressed. God what must he think of her. No wonder he questioned her decency. But who was he to pass judgment on her.

Fury fueled by guilt blurted out on Eve's tongue. "Malak you talk about decency, you're a fucking peeping Tom."

Silence hummed loudly throughout the room.

Malak realized Eve was fragile. He could read her shame and guilt all over her face. The belt of her trench coat unraveled. He stared back at the sexy voluptuous body and his thoughts raged thinking about Xavier touching her.

He stepped forward pulling her close. He felt the moment she relaxed into his embrace. He looked into her eyes. He was feeling mean for her having let Xavier touch her. "My God Eve you have no idea how much I want you. I guess you'll always be the kind of woman who has the good stuff that a man can't resist," he said curling his hand behind her head pulling her in close. He kissed her hard.

Eve shoved him away. "Stop you bastard, you're hurting me."

The moment was awkward.

"Look Eve, I'm sorry for that little move. Let's just call it even for your running back to Xavier.

Eve glanced up at Malak with a look of utter despair. "My love is not easy for any man to understand, let alone have. I don't run to any man, many men may say they love me, but it is always from afar."

Eve stared back at Malak as she watched him nervously pace the floor. She studied him intensely as her thoughts raced. Every minute she had spent with Malak she had known something was there. When had it grown to be the thing she felt deep in her heart?

Her voice caught in her throat. "How could you say you want me, but be with another woman?"

Nervously Malak ran his hands through his hair. "Damn it Eve. I know I should have told you, but she didn't mean anything to me. In fact, I was only at the ..."

"Get out!" Eve squeezed her eyes tighter trying to stop the tears.

"But Eve, you've got to let me explain?"

"No!"

Malak choked out pleading. "Listen Eve, once I tell you what really happened, you'll see I'm innocent, I promise you."

"I said get out! Get out! Get out!" She yelled turning and running from the room.

Chapter 19
That's what friends are for...

The next day the sun was surprisingly high overhead as Carina set off across the grass heading for the side gate. She opened the gate and a jungle of flowers and greenery, that was Eve's garden, met her eyes.

"Eve...Eve," she called out. "I know you're back here hiding Eve."

Eve sat under a tree in a white wicker love seat. She was dressed in torn blue jeans and a baby doll pajama top. She looked up as Carina walked near. "God you're a pest brat. You've got my key?"

"Yep, I've got it and I'm keeping it too. Why didn't you bother to take off your pajamas this morning? I bet you haven't even taken a shower."

"Good one brat. You're probably right. I wouldn't come any closer."

Carina walked over and sat beside her. She put her arms around her and gave her a hug.

The two friends sat together in silence for a moment.

Finally, Carina broke the ice. "You want to talk about it?"

"All men are dogs," Eve sobbed out.

"I know, but some of them can be trained."

Eve choked out a laugh. "Good one."

"So what do you want to do Eve? Declare war on Malak and win him back, or go over and beat him up?"

Eve sighed miserably. "You know I just keep hearing him say he wanted to explain. It was the way he said it, like he was trying to tell me the truth. Like he was innocent."

Carina sighed. "Okay then call up Malak and have him finish telling you what he was going to say."

"No I can't," Eve felt tears begin to grow. "I mean what if what he was really going to say was that he really likes her?"

Carina sighed heavily. She knew there was no point in trying to get Eve to see reason when she was like this. "Okay then, I'll just sit here with you and help you feel sorry for yourself."

Eve laughed. "That's why you're my best friend Carina. I love you like a sister."

Carina's face broke into a smile.

Eve gave her a hug.

It twisted Carina's heart to see Eve this way. She hugged her back. "Eve, have you ever thought that maybe Malak feels the same way that you do?"

"What do you mean? I'm not in love with Malak. I couldn't be. I mean I did know what love felt like a long time ago," her words caught in her thought. "I don't know why I'm telling you this. I vowed I never would. But I was in love a long time ago," she paused. "I was in love with Hawke. I thought I could never love again. But Malak makes me feel like I felt when I loved Hawke," she said with great sadness in her eyes.

"Eve, I'm your friend. Please let me help," Carina said, wanting to erase the sadness from her eyes. "Eve, don't you see you have a chance at love again with Malak?"

"Oh forget Malak. I'm putting him out of my mind. I've got to get over this and get back to my life."

Eve stood abruptly and turned away. She folded her arms as if she was protecting her heart as she strolled back to the house.

Carina watched Eve retreat. Her mind was stuck on Eve's sentence that Malak was going to tell her the truth.

All of a sudden Carina knew what needed to be done.

Chapter 20

A few days later, Eve was sure her heart would never mend.

She walked into the kitchen from the adjourning room determined to make a cup of tea. Normally she'd have a coffee. But since Carina had introduced her to the calming effects of tea, she needed a cup.

The sunshine yellow colors decorating the kitchen normally cheered her up. She smiled at the punches of red color that energized the room.

She placed the red tea kettle on the stove and waited for the pot to hum.

In a few minutes the tea kettle whistled and chirped and Eve made herself a large pot of chamomile tea.

Cupping the tea cup Eve walked back to her bedroom. She slowly breathed out content, as the warm tan, gold, and cream colors greeted her. She walked over to her large window and glanced out.

Slowly she sipped the warm brew and thought back over the night's events. She couldn't understand how things had gotten so out of control with Malak.

Instantly goose-bumps popped up on her arm. A strange frisson of something passed over her.

All at once, nasty laughter buzzed the air. "You thought you got rid of me the other night didn't you Eve? I don't know what you put on me. I've never slept that long before."

Eve jerked at the sound of Xavier's voice. "Oh my God, how did you get in here?"

"Didn't you know I have my own key Eve? You know how sweet little Carina is always leaving her key chain laying around. It was nothing for me to make a copy of your home key."

Eve was shaking. "Xavier, get out of my house now!"

He shook his head and closed the distance between them. "You don't want me to leave. You belong with me Eve," he ran his fingers through his hair and mumbled. "I can't understand it. You drank the passion fruit martini. You're supposed to feel something for me. That Glenda assured me it would work."

"What do you mean? I'm supposed to feel something for you?"

Eve couldn't believe her ears. All at once it dawned on her. She knew the only Glenda Xavier had to be talking about was Glenda D'Goodwrench-Jackson.

Xavier looked perplexed. "I…I…I don't know what you're talking about Eve."

"Don't tell me. Let me guess. Xavier you got a love potion from Glenda D'Goodwrench-Jackson and you had it put in that passion fruit martini at that party, right?"

"Eve you know I don't believe in that hocus pocus crap. I'm a college educated man," his voice pleaded.

Slowly he stepped closer, carefully sensing her mood. He needed to take her mind off of her thoughts. He smiled and softly said. "You are love, pleasure and desire. That's why Malak can't get you out of his mind."

He inched closer. Gently his hand reached out and cupped her chin. All at once he pulled back as if sensing something.

"There's something different about you Eve."

Eve thought she heard a noise. She wondered if Xavier heard it too. "What?"

"Yes, I can tell. He's been touching you. I can smell Malak all over you. Where the hell is Malak? You've been fucking him haven't you Eve?"

Eve tried to push out of his embrace. "You bastard. How dare you speak to me like that?"

Xavier's dark eyes glittered with jealously. "I asked you a question woman! Did you fuck him?"

Eve twisted trying to defy him. She raised her hand trying to slap his face.

Xavier grabbed her wrist and pulled her closer. His erection throbbed against her. He took her hand and forced it to his cock. "Do you feel that? That's how much I want you?"

"No," Eve said panting down a sob.

Eve fought back. She hit him and tried to scratch his eyes out.

Xavier laughed out. "That's it Eve fight me. Fight me back. You look beautiful doing that."

"You bastard!"

His sadistic laugh echoed.

Eve stared back at Xavier and realized he was enjoying every minute of her humiliation. Somewhere in the deep recesses of her mind she saw the strong woman that she was. She couldn't let him hurt her or steal her sense of self.

She thought she heard that noise again.

Eve met his gaze. With a deep awareness she remembered who she was. She knew what she had to do. She realized she would never let him touch her. She stared back at him fearing nothing. She smiled back at Xavier like the cat that caught the mouse. "Xavier I don't think you could fuck me better than Malak does. But go ahead and give it your best shot."

"What?" He said releasing his grip on her wrists.

Xavier looked at her in stunned disbelief.

All at once she laughed loudly. "I don't think Malak will be very nice to you once he realized you've tried to have sex with his woman. You're a fool Xavier if you think Malak will ever let you get away with it."

Xavier hissed under his breath. He needed to take control. "Stop lying bitch. You don't belong to Malak. How can you when you don't even know his secret."

"I know about Aaliyah Mondragon and how you blackmailed her to set Malak up so I'd see the two of them together. I even found out my seeing them kissing at just the right time, was also staged by you Xavier!"

"Malak is a liar. See how little you know about the man. I told you before he wasn't any good for you. You should have listened to me."

For a long moment Eve just stared back at Xavier frozen. She could tell he was just trying to gain control over her.

Her eyes greedily fastened on her bedroom door. She noticed the door was ajar.

"What is it this time Xavier?" She asked defiantly.

"Aaliyah isn't the secret. His being Hawke Deville is the secret."

"I heard that. It's true!" Hawke's voice sliced the air. "Now get your hands off of my lady!"

Xavier looked like a weasel caught in a trap. He seemed to shrink from the presence of Malak entering the room.

"Damn did she have you hiding in her closet?"

Behind Malak, Carina's voice rang out. "The party is over for you Xavier, you idiot. Unless you think I was hiding in the closet too."

"Shut up Carina. Damn I hate you Carina. You are always meddling in, where Eve is concerned."

Quietly Eve edged away from Xavier.

Furious Xavier reached out and grabbed Eve by the hair. "Bitch, get back here," his face marred in a deep snarl. "Stay back Hawke. Or I'll declare war on you and your woman."

Carina screamed.

Hawke laughed out. His voice is brawling, brash and vigorous. "Why hurt Eve. I always thought you just wanted to get revenge on me? he asked but didn't wait for an answer. "Well now is your chance to fight me man to man. Or will you get a bigger kick out of hurting a woman?"

Furious, Xavier looked back at Hawke. "I did get revenge on you. I got you father to send you away, didn't I? He always thought it was you that stole that money."

Hawke gave Eve a wink. "Well now that the old gangs all here. How about I tell a little story, huh Xavier?"

Xavier fixed Hawke with a stare. "No one will believe your stories Hawke Deville or do you prefer Malak?"

Hawke laughed. "You never were too bright Xavier. Malak is one of my middle names. But, let me tell the story. You see once upon a time a girl named Eve was in love with a boy name Hawke. The boy named Hawke was madly in love with the girl but he was too foolish to tell her. Then at *The Grand Isles* Christmas Ball the girl got her courage up and told the boy. The two of them ended up in bed together. Unbeknownst to the two of them a villainous, manipulative, selfish scoundrel watched them and he plotted and planned."

"Hawke you forget to use the word pimp," Carina added.

"Shut up Carina," Xavier snapped.

"To make a long story short," Hawke's gaze settled on Eve's face. "There was a boy who was betrayed by his friend. The friend was a true to life villain. This villain got the boy's father to believe his son had stolen a large sum of money from his father. But that wasn't the worst of it. This villain told the boy's father he'd gotten a girl pregnant," he said pausing and shaking his head. His voice caught in his throat.

Eve's heart shot up into her throat. Her lower lip trembled. "Hawke," his name came out in a choked cry. "Please finish your story."

Hawke shifted his stance. "The father sent his son away to boarding school. Sometime after that the girl miscarried. She lost their baby. But only a few of her closest friends knew that, including the villain, and none of them spoke of it. So the boy never knew the girl was pregnant until many years later. By then there was no way he could bring the subject up to the girl to tell her how sorry he was. Because, by then the villain had tainted the girls mind to believe bad thoughts about the boy," you see this villain had plans to have the girl all for himself."

Eve swallowed hard. Tears clogged her throat and shimmered in her eyes. "Is that all the story?"

"No, the Boy never stopped loving the girl. In fact he is still crazy about the girl," he sighed. "But let me finish the story. In time all truths were revealed and the boy finally got the chance to tell the girl he was sorry. Because he was still in love with the girl and he had to do whatever it took so that she would know."

Hawke gave Eve a knowing wink. "Thanks for letting me tell you my story Eve."

Eve held her head high and smiled back at him. "And I believe your story Malak…I mean Hawke and I accept your apology. I never blamed you." She shook her head. "My heart always belonged to you. I'm crazy about you. Every bit of you, especially that beard."

Xavier sneered. "Damn, you're a melodrama queen Eve. That wasn't called for. Hawke's a bad guy period, end of story. Now I'll stop being mister nice guy," he murmured leaned over and whispered. His breath did something to her sense. He reached out and cupped her chin. "Look at me Eve. I'm going to take you where your true feelings are. You are in love with me," he commanded.

Eve had no perception of time. She felt her heart flutter and beat erratically. Her feelings were conflicting. She felt like only the room was empty except for Xavier. She could see Xavier's mouth moving. White mist moved in front of her eyes. She realized Xavier was casting some kind of spell. Wasn't this just how this all started, with a love potion.

The light in the room seemed to change. It seemed like a long dark tunnel.

Suddenly an overpowering smell whiffed the air. It smelled like the fragrant smell of the Berkley Bart station. "Oh how I wished Glenda D'Goodwrench-Jackson was here. She could undo what hold Xavier has put on me," she stammered slowly. "Glenda D'Goodwrench-Jackson, Glenda D'Goodwrench-Jackson, Glenda D'Goodwrench-Jackson," she murmured over and over again.

A brilliant light flashed.

All at once Glenda D'Goodwrench-Jackson whipped out of thin air. She waved her hand with the large ruby ring, harnessing power from the air. "Look at me Eve," she commanded. "All you have to do is touch your pendant. You can change everything just touch your pendant Eve!"

Quickly Eve's fingers touched her pendant. She felt like lightning bolts of pulsating energy came to her through the pendant. It came from the sky, the heavens, the earth, she was protected. She felt it.

Eve got her courage up and looked up into Xavier's face. She stared him down like high noon at the Ok corral. As she did she slowly inched away from him. "Hawke isn't the bad guy you are Xavier. You're what my mother used to call a *Deceiver*. I can't believe I've been so easily deceived by you all these years. And now I know the truth."

In an instant the illusion of the beautiful loving moment was shattered in the blink of an eye.

Xavier reached out and grabbed her arm. His free hand reached high up into the air.

"What do you want to do? Hit me Xavier? I heard you like to hit women. Hit me Xavier,' Eve said as her face contorted into an old woman's. "I swear everyone will know what you are."

"Grandmother?" Xavier hung his head. The smug grin died on his face. He dropped his hand and stepped back.

Eve stared back at him. In an instance she jumped out of his reach.

In the nick of time Hawke moved in and took her place.

"Fine Eve I'll show you. I fight men. I'm not a lady hitter. Who told you that crap anyway? I bet it was that whore Layla Moon, from the party. I saw her talking to you at your car. That bitch owed me money. She deserved what I did to her. I'll kick your man's ass now. I'll show you what kind of man I am."

Xavier closed the distance with Hawke. He couldn't wait to make Hawke pay for sleeping with Eve. He hissed out. "Come on Hawke. I should have kicked your ass that night I caught you at Eve's house, that night after *The Grand Isles* Christmas Ball. "

Hawke squared his shoulders and stood erect.

Xavier threw a punch it made contact and Hawke's head flew back. He went crashing to the floor.

"Well Hawke, do you still feel like fighting me?"

Hawked gazed back at him silently and quickly got up off of the floor. He readied himself and moved in closer. Ready to do battle he threw a surprise overhand right. He came back with a left to the side of the head. He brought in an uppercut.

Xavier staggered back.

Hawke moved in closer again. He landed several punches again. He followed them with a big upper cut.

Xavier staggered again, this time his knees buckled and then they gave out. He went down for the count.

Eve rushed over. "Oh Hawke are you okay? I can't believe you fought for me."

Hawke's eyes gleamed with desire for her. "Eve, you're not angry that I'm Hawke and not Malak are you?"

Tears of joy glistened in her eyes. She pressed her fingers to his lips. "Hawke Malak Deville it's you I want to be with. I always have and I always will."

His large hand cupped her check and he kissed her.

Eve put her hands around his neck.

They heard a rustling noise and turned around.

Carina held a small plastic bag and reached down touching Xavier. His body jerked.

"Carina! What are you doing?

Don't zap the man with a stun gun when he's already down," Hawke scolded.

Carina stood up and shrugged. "It's not a stun gun. I just touched him with a little bit of this dust. I want to make sure he can't hurt Eve ever again."

"Dust? I don't think I want to know what you're talking about Carina."

Eve close the gap between her and her friend. "Carina, I want to know where you got the dust from. Its graveyard dust isn't it? You know you shouldn't mess with that Louisiana hocus pocus stuff. Whose is it anyway?"

"Don't worry Eve. It's from the grave of a person that asked that it be used to keep Xavier in check," Carina said.

Eve shook her head. "It must have come from his grandmother's grave. When I thought he was going to hit me. All at once he looked at me funny and called me grandmother."

Carina looked between Eve and Hawke. "Did you know Xavier Newhouse and Grant Godeau shared a grandmother? They're cousins you know. Grant told me all about her. Did you know she kept a keepsake book? He showed it to me," she paused. "In it she had a letter telling all about how bad Xavier was and what he was capable of. She said she knew once she died, no one in the family could ever keep Xavier in check so she left specific instructions for Grant telling him what he needed to know. Grant has a bag of her graveyard dirt in a safe."

Eve's brow rose. "And you borrowed some?"

"Yes I did," Carina said. "You always looked out for me, when we were kids. I figured it was time I paid you back. You need someone to look out for you sometimes."

Eve felt proud. Her eyes held a gleam of tears.

Carina turned and eyed Hawke. "By the way Hawke I knew it was you all alone. You can dye your hair, wear a beard and wear contacts lenses all you want but I'd still know that geeky smile of yours anywhere. You'd better take really good care of my best friend."

Carina turned to Eve and gave her friend a big hug. "Well Eve looks like the Angels lead you to your geek and you caught the deceiver red handed," she grinned. "This has the makings of a great movie. I can't wait to tell Grant."

The two best friends laughed.

Hawke spoke up. "Carina I owe you, thanks for telling Eve about Aaliyah Mondragon."

Carina fixed her gaze on her hands and inspected her fingernails. Nervously she chuckled as if giving the matter barely a second thought. "I was very happy to help. Once I found out what was really going on. I couldn't rest until I knew the truth. How else would Eve know that Xavier was black mailing Aaliyah to set you up so that she would catch the two of you together?"

Hawke gazed at her with thankful eyes. He turned his attention to Eve and gave her a loving hug.

Epilogue
December Wedding Why not...

The Deville Estate was ablaze with lights. Sparkling lights covered every tree and bush leading to the estate. Inside the massive foyer a tall Christmas tree stood to one side, decorated beautifully with gold and ivory ornaments. The house was decorated lavishly with fresh flowers in every nook and corner.

Eve smiled, watching Carina adjust the tiara veil on her head. Tendrils of Eve's hair curled softly just behind her ear, where pearl and diamond teardrop earrings flashed brilliantly.

"Gosh, you are a beautiful bride Eve."

"And don't worry Carina. I won't lose your diamond and pearl earrings. Thanks for letting me borrow them."

A loud knock sounded on the bedroom door. Grant's voice sliced through the door. "Ladies this ceremony needs to get started. I have an anxious groom wondering where his bride is."

Carina laughed out. "We are on our way Grant. Start the music."

৪০৪০৪০

An hour later, the ceremony was beautiful. It was everything Eve had ever dreamed of.

The minister's voice was stern when he asked. "Do you Hawke Malak Antony Deville take this woman Eve Chastity Lafoy to be your lawful wife?"

"I do."

Eve's eyes filled with tears and her hand trembled when Hawke placed the diamond platinum wedding band on her finger.

"We are now man and wife Eve. The minister said so," he smiled back at her. So tell me Mrs. Deville, what will be first on your first honey do task list for your husband?"

"The First thing I require is for you to kiss me like this each and every day."

"Stop that kissing you two," Grant said. He swept the two newlyweds in his arms. "Come on cousins. We have a reception to attend. There are a couple hundred relatives and friends waiting to be fed, including me," he joked.

Laughter spilled from Eve's lips. "I love this man. I love him. I love him," she smiled.

Hawke's mouth covered hers in a kiss that left them both trembling. "I love you too Eve, always and forever," he grinned.

Finally, Hawke noticed Grant standing there and he pulled out of her embrace.

Hawke eyes sparkled. "Say cousin," he smiled. "After we finish eating, do me a big favor and help Eve and me escape. I've got the honeymoon suite booked at the Fairmont Hotel."

Grant grinned. "You can count on me cousin."

"And me," Carina said walking in close. "Now let's eat. You two are trying to starve Grant and me to death."

Eve's arms circled Hawke's arm. "We don't need food. Love is all that matters."

Hawke smiled hungrily. "Come on woman. A man's got to have food too."

The couple walked off laughing joyfully.

The End

Coming Soon...

Lovers, Players, The Seducer Book II

Revenge

Last time, in J. A. Jackson's steamy, romantic thriller *Lovers, Players and The Seducer*, the storm came...and went.

Back then, Nicholas La Cour played a very dangerous game of cat and mouse; one in which he involved his childhood friends, Kienan Egan and Quinn Rolandis. Even worse, he put his own sister, Lacey La Cour, right in the middle of that storm.

Everyone got swept away in the torrent of greed, lust and ruthless ambition. All except two ratchet lovers...

Another storm is coming, but will the two ratchet lovers survive it? Find out in Jackson's anticipated sequel, *Lovers, Players The Seducer*, Book II *THE REVENGE GAME*. Winner takes all.

About the Author J. A. JACKSON

J.A. JACKSON is an author who lives in an enchanted little house she calls home in the Northern California foothills with her husband and Big Sally an American scent hound. She fell in love with writing as a small child. She was born in Arkansas and comes from a family rich in story tellers. She spent over ten years working in the non-profit sector where she wrote grants, press releases and contributed many stories to their newsletter. She was their Newsletter editor for over ten years. She loves growing roses, a good pot of hot tea, chocolate, magical stories, suspense stories, ghost stories, and reading Jane Austen again and again in her past time. Please write her at P.O. Box 612751 San Jose, CA 9516.Email Address: **jerreecejackson@gmail.com jerreecejackson@yahoo.com**

Discover all the deliciously Romantic, Suspenseful, and Entertaining Novels by author J. A. Jackson, each with unique surprises and something for every reader here!
https://www.amazon.com/author/jajackson

Dear Gentle Readers

Dear Gentle Readers, Fans, Family and Friends,
Reviews for my books are what this author needs… Let me explain.

In an effort to provide you with the most honest information about me. I confess I am a self-published author.
That's right, I am committed to writing a story, a novel every chance I get (hopefully I will put out two to three books a year). Even though I have a whacked-out, frenetic, hectic schedule as do many others. I persevere. I am committed to writing my stories.
With that said, I'd like to make a request of you my gentle readers, followers, friends, and family. I appreciate that you read my books. And I need you to please go to Amazon.com or KINDLE and review my book.
I will be truthful if you do. I would like for you to help me. Your kindness to me in reviewing my books would go a long way in helping me continue my self-publishing journey.

Thank you for all that you do. I truly appreciate you!
Sincerely,
J. A. Jackson
Email: jerreecejackson@gmail.com

Books by J. A. Jackson

❀ *A Geek an Angel Series*

The Deceiver
The Proposition
The Grand Hotel
Lovers, Players, & The Seducer
Lovers, Players, Revenge

❀ *The Mistress of Desire*
& The Orchid Lover

❀ *When* A Taker *Dreams*

Book Links

Lovers, Players & The Seducer
http://www.amazon.com/dp/B00ARCEGHJA

The Mistress of Desire & The Orchid Lover
http://www.amazon.com/dp/B00ND6HV3C

The Grand Hotel
http://www.amazon.com/dp/B00CLF7JU6

The Deceiver
http://www.amazon.com/dp/B009Q6ICH2

The Proposition
http://www.amazon.com/dp/B00BE6EQT0

Thank you for all that you do.

I truly appreciate you!

www.ingramcontent.com/pod-product-compliance
Lightning Source LLC
Chambersburg PA
CBHW060432130626
46555CB00005B/2318